A Journey Beyond Silence

A Journey Beyond Silence

A Story of Hearing Loss

Elometer Victoria Thomas

iUniverse, Inc.
New York   Bloomington

iUniverse books may be ordered through booksellers or by contacting:

iUniverse
1663 Liberty Drive
Bloomington, IN 47403
www.iuniverse.com
1-800-Authors (1-800-288-4677)

Because of the dynamic nature of the Internet, any Web addresses or links contained in
this book may have changed since publication and may no longer be valid. The views
expressed in this work are solely those of the author and do not necessarily reflect the
views of the publisher, and the publisher hereby disclaims any responsibility for them.

ISBN: 978-1-4401-7543-5 (sc)
ISBN: 978-1-4401-7542-8 (dj)
ISBN: 978-1-4401-8287-7 (ebook)

Printed in the United States of America

iUniverse rev. date: 10/30/2009

To my family,
who mean more to me
than anything in the world

Contents

Preface

MY CHIEF AIM for writing about my experiences in both a hearing and a silent world is to show hearing loss in a different perspective from the way the world sees it. There is too much misunderstanding and too much prejudice associated with hearing loss. I have felt compelled to give my views in the hope that my experience will help others to understand the stark horror that accompanies the loss of sounds.

As a child growing up in a hearing world where all my playmates were hearing children, I desperately wanted my family and friends to accept me as a normal person. This turned out to be one of the biggest battles of my life. I knew my family meant well, but they had no experience with hearing loss. Perhaps they did not realize that I was still the same person inside. I wanted to go back to school and be like all my playmates; instead, I was kept in isolation, shut away from the world. My family insisted that other children would make fun of me if I went back to school. By the time I was fourteen, I began to realize that the biggest barrier in my life and the lives of others like me was not deafness but the public view of deafness. The feelings of alienation were more painful for me than the hearing loss itself.

As I tell this story, I realize that there are more than thirty million Americans living with hearing loss. Millions of them live in seclusion because they do not have a voice in a world geared for the hearing. It is unimaginably hard for a child born deaf to learn a language he or she has never heard. We should all be aware that deaf children—especially those born deaf—have never heard our voices and therefore have never heard the words they should reproduce. We could never go to a foreign country and speak a language we have never heard before—even though we are able to hear others speak it. Few of us realize that 90 percent of deaf children are born to hearing parents. It's a sad fact that deafness and hearing loss affect all segments of society, all over the world. Communication barriers mean that hearing loss is poorly understood. Millions of people with hearing loss stand on the doorsteps of the world, hoping to find a way to communicate in a world geared for the hearing.

My story is your story. It's a story that so many of you can relate to. It's the story of every individual who has had to struggle with the obstacles and trials of life. But it is also a story of hope, carrying the message that despair can be overcome. It's a testimony to the durability and determination of every human being who struggles to find happiness against hopelessness. I hope my experience will give others the courage and inspiration to do what they know is right.

Acknowledgments

MANY THANKS TO the iUniverse publishing company for giving me the opportunity to publish this book. Thanks also to the wonderful people at iUniverse, especially Randall Gillette, publishing consultant, and Cathy Raymond, editorial consultant, for giving me valuable advice. I am very grateful to Steve Furr for his assistance in resolving technical and computer problems. Thanks also to the editors and the customer support team for their help throughout the publishing process.

Thanks to my wonderful son, Mark, for his endless patience. If it weren't for the long hours Mark spent helping me, I would never have been able to understand the workings of the computer, which had me very frustrated!

I must also thank my wonderful daughter, Anne, and my ever-loving brother, Val, for their confidence and encouragement. Thank you for being so patient over the years and for not giving up on me.

And finally, I must give thanks to God for giving me the courage and inspiration to write and finish this book.

CHAPTER 1

A Beginning and an End

B RIGHT SUNSHINE GREETED me as my father led me out of the hospital corridor and into a waiting horse-drawn carriage. After three months of isolation in a lonely hospital room, longing to see my family and friends, I was happy that at last I was finally going home.

During the long ride home from the hospital, I fell asleep and woke up to find a hand lifting me and carrying me into my grandparents' home. The room was crowded with relatives, and knowing I was home, I suddenly felt awake. As each of my relatives came forward to hug and greet me, I sensed something was wrong. No one was saying anything to me, and there wasn't a sound in the room. I remember Grandma coming toward me and bending over me; as I gazed into her face, I realized that her lips were moving and I tried to make sense of what she was saying, but I wasn't hearing anything.

Little did I know that I was about to embark on a long and painful journey into a silent world of no return.

I was born in Flagaman, a rural district in the parish of St. Elizabeth, on the island of Jamaica. In the 1940s, Flagaman and the surrounding district was a predominantly fair-skinned population. It was commonly believed that we were the descendant of European settlers.

My earliest childhood memories include my mother and my ten-year-old sister, Doris. We were then living in a tiny one-bedroom house that my father was building for us. My memories of those early years include some of the most traumatic events in my life: the sudden death of my mother, the separation from my sister, and the relocation from our home. My memory of my mother, Evadney, is somewhat blurred by the years. Unfortunately, I have no photograph of her, but I remember her as a beautiful woman who always wore her straight dark hair parted in the center. Even today, after all these years, I can still remember her wonderful singing voice, as she tucked me into bed at night, Little Anita, she called me.

My happy life with my mother came to an abrupt end early one morning when I was awakened by the sound of someone screaming. A large crowd had gathered in front of our little home, crying, "She is dead. She is gone, gone, gone."

Needless to say, as a five-year-old I was much too young to know what all the commotion was about. I had never seen so many grown-ups crying, and I was curious to know what had happened. I remember someone picking me up and carrying me away from the home. Later, I woke up to find myself in my paternal grandparents' home, a place that was unfamiliar to me. I didn't know how I had gotten there.

When my father took me back to our home, I saw that a large crowd had assembled there. Outside the front door was a large mahogany box supported by two chairs. Dad lifted me up so I could see inside. Mom was lying in the box, dressed in white. She looked beautiful, just as she always did when she was asleep. The wind was gently blowing her hair away from her forehead. I knew nothing about death and believed that my mother was asleep and that she would wake up and come back to my sister and me.

I can't recall what happened afterward, and I don't remember anything about the funeral. I do remember being told that I would have to stay with my father and his parents, whom I barely knew at the time. I couldn't stop crying when I was told that my mother had gone away and that my sister, Doris, had gone to stay with Aunt Bertha (Mom's sister).

It was not until several years later that I learned of my mother's struggles to support my sister and me as a single parent and of her sudden, tragic, and untimely death after giving birth to my brother, Valney.

My parents were never married, and my father, G. Ambrose Ebanks, never lived with us. He was still living with his parents, John and Florence Ebanks, when I came to live with them. His three brothers, Reggie, Easton, Everett, and a sister, Vie, all lived with their parents in a modest three-bedroom house on a farm. It was a huge farm, known locally as Sea Breeze. What I remember most about the home was the beautiful mahogany floor. On hot summer days, I loved to lie on the cool floor until I fell asleep. The farm had numerous fruit trees of every kind. When no one was looking, I would climb the trees and pick the fruit—and hide them. My favorite was the grape vine; its grapes were my favorite fruit. The farm was well protected from outsiders by a barbed-wire fence and two enormous iron gates.

With his parents and three brothers, Dad made a comfortable living farming the land. Dad's family were successful farmers who bred cows, goats, pigs, and chickens. They hired many local people to work on their farm.

The farm was remote, and we didn't have electricity, but neither did any of our neighbors. At night, the countryside was very dark, and we had to light kerosene lamps or storm lanterns as soon as the sun went down. The nearest main road was more than two miles away, and very few people in the district owned cars. Most of our neighbors got around on horseback, by bicycle, or on foot.

The first few weeks with my grandparents were agony for me. I missed my mother and my sister. At night, I was afraid of the dark. Scared of sleeping alone, I remember lying awake for hours, listening to all kinds of sounds in the stillness of the night, including the constant barking of my grandparents' dogs.

It didn't take long for me to adjust to living at Sea Breeze, though. It was like discovering a huge playground. Soon I was out playing hide-and-seek with my four-year- old cousin Audley, the son of Uncle Sydney, Dad's brother, whom Grandma had adopted when he was two years old. My other playmates at the time were mainly the children of my aunts and uncles and other children from the neighborhood. We played hopscotch, jumped rope, climbed trees, and played an endless array of games. I was quite a tomboy in those days: I could outrace everyone, and there wasn't a tree on my grandparents' property that I couldn't climb. But for me, the main attraction at Sea Breeze was the hills and the caves where we played hide-and-seek. Sometimes we would stand outside and yell, "Hello" to the caves, which was a short distance from our home. Then we'd pause and listen for the echo of our voices coming back. The echo of our voices from the caves was the most exciting sound in the world for me.

Climbing the hills was another challenge. We would climb to the top on one side and then try to get down on the other side. Sometimes, completely exhausted, I would lie in the cool, lush, green grass that grew in abundance around our home and listen to the singing of the birds as they fluttered from one branch of a tree to another. Then there was the stable. Uncle Reggie, Dad's older brother—tall, slim, and blond—sometimes took us horseback riding. I can well remember the first time he took a group of us cousins to the beach. I had never been to a beach before, and it was an exciting experience for me. Even before we neared the ocean, I could see and hear the mighty waves lapping against the rocks. I loved the wonderful feeling of swimming with the waves washing over me.

My life was filled with excitement and wonder then; writing about that time evokes many good memories. I can vividly recall the voices of my family and playmates, the sound of music, the sound of the wind and the rain, and the endless different sounds that filled my life.

Grandma, as I came to call my father's mother, was a tall, slim, attractive woman with dark curly hair. She was in her fifties but looked much younger. A strong-willed woman, she was very strict. I noticed that she made all the rules in the family. My grandfather, on the other hand, was a big, quiet man, whom everyone called JB. I must have been the only one who called him Grandpa.

Unlike the other adults in the home, Grandpa JB often came out to play games with my cousins and me. We all adored him because he was so big and funny.

I well remember the day Grandma told me that I had a baby brother. I was sitting outside watching some of my cousins playing when she came and sat beside me. "I have a surprise for you," she said as she took my hands and led me back into the house. My heart was pounding as I wondered what the surprise would be. Once inside, Grandma went straight to the bed where Valney (we all called him Val), the new baby, was sleeping. "This baby is your baby brother, your mother's baby," Grandma said. I was curious. I had always been told that babies came from heaven, and I wanted to ask Grandma where the baby came from. I was confused too: not only did I not know where my mother was, I didn't know that my mother had a baby.

I soon took a keen interest in my mother's baby. I wanted to help Grandma feed him, change him, burp him, and rock him, but she wouldn't let me. Incredibly, this didn't bother me for too long; like most children my age, I simply accepted things as they were.

As a child I loved music, dancing, and singing. Although we didn't have a radio or TV in our home, we never lacked for music. Many of the local boys went around the neighborhood in groups, playing guitar, banjo, trumpet, or drums. Music was a big part of my life, especially the drums.

They produced an exhilarating sound and created a wonderful vibration that I felt through my whole body.

I didn't see much of my father during this time, but I noticed that he always left the house when the sun began to set. I always wondered where he went; he was always well dressed when he went out. One evening I noticed that Dad was dressed and ready to leave. I'll never know what made me decide to follow him. I kept a good distance away from him so that he couldn't hear my footsteps. I didn't want him to know that I was following him; I simply wanted to find out where he was going. After following him for what seemed a long time, I wanted to turn back, but I continued on until Dad turned a corner. Suddenly, I heard the barking of dogs, and out of the bushes sprang two big dogs running in my direction. I turned on my heels and ran as fast as I could, all the way back home. I was terrified and my heart was pounding violently. I knew it had been a foolish thing to do, so I didn't tell anyone, but it was a traumatic lesson for me. Shortly afterward, I began having nightmares about dogs barking and running after me. I had those dreams so often that I would lie awake for hours, not wanting to go back to sleep. One night, after one of those frightening dreams, I was unable to sleep and afraid of the darkness around me. I heard the sound of an owl and then rustling in the trees. The owl seemed to be coming close to the window. Fear gripped me and I began to sob quietly, not wanting to wake anyone.

I heard Grandma's voice in the next room ask, "What's the matter, darling?"

"I can't sleep," I sobbed "I dreamed that two dogs were barking and running after me."

"Well, dear," she said, "it's only a dream. Now go back to sleep."

"No," I sobbed, "I am going to dream the same thing all over again."

Her voice was soothing and calm when she replied, "Nita, dear, I promise you will never dream that again." She went on, "No one ever dreams the same dream in one night."

I must have had complete confidence in Grandma, for after that, I never had those dreams again.

My father's only sister, Aunt Vie, was blind. I noticed that she never went anywhere. "She can't see a thing." I overheard one of the neighbors saying. "If she goes outside, she will bounce into a tree."

I was amazed that she could get around inside the home without bumping into the furniture. My first impression was that she must have had some wonderful sixth sense to guide her, since she never used a cane. We kids would sneak in and out of the house, hoping she wouldn't recognize us. But I soon realized that she could easily detect which family members were going and coming by the sound of our footsteps.

I was almost seven when Grandma began taking Audley and me to St. Peter Anglican Church dressed in our Sunday best. I loved the singing and the music from the harp and the piano. I always wished that Grandma would take Aunt Vie with us. I remember feeling sorry for Aunt Vie because no one in the family ever took her anywhere with them. I would look at Aunt Vie and wonder how awful she must have felt, confined to the house, unable to see the world or go anywhere.

After the church service, Grandma often took us to visit our relatives; a different one each Sunday. I lived for those visits. I loved to visit my mother's father, Jonathan. Dada, as I called him, was a tall, gray-haired man who was always happy to see me. Each time I visited, he would sit me on his lap and read me wonderful stories. One day, he told me about my mother and said how much I looked like her when she was my age. "Your mommy was beautiful, just like you, she would be so happy to see you now." He said. I always felt that if my mother had lived to see me grow up, we would have been the best of friends, and my life probably would have taken a different turn.

Around this time I began running errands, mostly to Aunt Bertha, who lived on the farm next to us. It was just a ten minutes' walk and I didn't mind. Grandma would hand me a cup and say, "Go over to Bertha's and borrow some sugar," or borrow some flour, borrow some salt, borrow a grater. The list was endless. Perhaps that's how I got the nickname "Errand Gal Sarah." I hated the name because it was the name of an old woman who went around the neighborhood with a cane, begging for food.

At seven I started school. Like most children in Jamaica, I had no preschool education then. But then, in the 1940s, many children grew up without any schooling at all. There were no kindergartens, and children had to be seven years old or older to be accepted into school. Perdo Plains, the only school serving our area and several districts, was more than two miles away.

My first day of school was an exhilarating experience. I didn't mind walking the two miles to get there. I had always admired my big sister, Doris, and my cousin Angela, who was Aunt Bertha's daughter. Doris and Angela were bigger girls whom I adored, and I felt protected going to school with them. I had fun walking to school with a group of other kids. We skipped along and told funny stories until we reached the school. At school, I met other children from different parts of the district and made many new friends. I also learned a lot of new games.

Angela had a wonderful singing voice, and I wanted so much to be like her. She had a beautiful name, almost like an angel. To top it off, she had two wonderful parents at home who loved her so much and gave her everything she wanted. Like my sister Doris, Angela had flawless, smooth skin, and beautiful dark brown hair.

As for me, I didn't like my name or my hair, which was very curly. Kids at school constantly teased me about having such a funny name. As far as

I was concerned, it was just a name on my birth certificate. Fortunately, no one in my family ever called me Elometer; I was always Nita or Anita to my family and playmates.

In those days we didn't have a clock or watch in our home, but I quickly learned some tricks to guess the time. Angela told me one day that if we were late for classes, the teacher would use a belt to strap us. She did her best to teach me all the tricks to get to school on time. One day, we were running along, thinking we were late. We were a short distance from the school when Angela held me back. "We are not late," she said.

"How do you know?"

"Didn't you hear that, Nita?" she asked.

I stopped and listened. In the distance, I heard something scraping across the concrete floor of the school. "Sounds like the benches moving," I said.

"They are arranging the benches," Angela corrected me. "It means we are on time."

The next day, we were almost at the school when we heard the ringing of the school bell. We hurried and got into the waiting line just in time.

I was equally happy in the classroom or at recess. I loved the challenge of spelling, and it came pretty easily to me. In a couple of weeks, I had progressed from spelling simple three-letter words to reading and writing short sentences. My learning ability seemed to impress my teacher, Miss Adlin, my family, and everyone in the school. Toward the end of the three-month school term, I was very surprised when my teacher informed my family that she would be placing me two grades ahead of my class. This was good news for me, but I was not so happy when the teacher called our class together to announce the ending of the school term.

"Children," she said. "Remember what I told you last week? School will be closed tomorrow for Easter."

All around me the children were happily clapping, glad to be out of school. I was clapping, but somehow I knew I was going to miss school. I was having so much fun that I never wanted it to end. When the clapping subsided, the teacher went on, "All of you kids who have a passing grade will be going to a new class." When my name was called, she stepped forward and hugged me. "Congratulations, Ellie!" (Miss Adlin had given me the nickname, which made me very happy.) "I am sorry I am not going to be your teacher anymore. You have done so well in reading, I am sending you to the first grade. I will really miss you."

I was too stunned to say anything. Getting to first grade after only three months seemed impossible. "I will miss you too, Miss. Adlin," I finally managed to say.

I had no idea of the fate awaiting me. I didn't know it then, but that day was to be the last day of school in my entire life.

Once out of school, I couldn't wait to get back to my school friends. I was thrilled to know I was going back to a new grade. I also enjoyed the wonderful freedom of being out in the open air, racing around the farm with my cousins, Audley, Angie and Seymour, and sometimes with our dogs Dick and Rocksavage.

Unfortunately, after only a few days, Grandma began sending me once again on errands almost daily. Sometimes she sent me to the home of my Aunt Lulu, my mother's sister, who was married to Uncle Sydney, my father's brother.

Aunt Lulu was always my favorite aunt. I didn't mind visiting her, but she lived more than two miles away, and the roads between Grandma's and Aunt Lulu's home were hilly and perilous, covered with thorns and bushes, and rocks. Even today, I find it hard to believe that I was able to travel alone on such a perilous path. Often, I heard the sound of wild animals in the bushes. I was often exhausted and covered with cuts and scratches after those trips. Sometimes, though, I was allowed to spend a couple of days at Aunt Lulu's house before returning home to Grandma's.

In those days, as far as I can remember, our family celebrated only three holidays: Christmas, New Year's, and Easter. I can still remember that second Easter I spent with my grandparents. The crowing of the rooster woke me up early that morning, and I didn't go back to sleep as I usually did. It was broad daylight as I walked out to the stable, the cool morning air whipping at my thin nightdress. I stood in a corner of the stable away from the wind and watched as Uncle Reggie let the horse out to pasture.

"Uncle," I called out. "Can I have a ride?"

He turned and looked at me surprised. Obviously he didn't know I was standing there.

"What are you doing up so early?" he asked.

"The rooster woke me up," I said. "I couldn't go back to sleep."

I laughed as he began mimicking the rooster. Then he looked down at me in my nightdress and said, "You know how silly you will look riding a horse in that thing?"

I rushed back inside the house and quickly changed into a dress. (We were never allowed to wear pants in Grandma's house.) When I got back to the stable, Uncle Reggie was already in the saddle. Disappointed, I watched as he rode off. In a few minutes, though, he came back to where I was standing.

"Ready, little girl?" he shouted down at me.

I ran toward him, and he pulled me up beside him. I remember holding tightly onto his clothes as the horse trotted away, slowly, at first, then in a gallop. It felt so wonderful to be up and away in the open air with the cool breeze howling in my ears and whipping at my face. I am not sure how long we rode, but I must have relaxed my hold, for the next thing I knew, I had fallen into the soft grass. As I got to my feet, I was shaking like a leaf but didn't think I was hurt. Mercifully, I suffered no bruises or scratches; but I was scared and my hands were trembling.

A few minutes later, I was back in the house, everything about the fall forgotten. I heard Grandma calling to me from the kitchen. "Nita," she stood in the doorway, a basket in her hands. "I need you. I want you to take this basket of corn to your Aunt Lulu—she wants it for Easter."

I looked at the basket of corn in her hands, and suddenly I felt weak in the knees. Going through the hills and bushes was hard enough. How could Grandma expect me to keep my balance without using my two hands to climb those hills? My first impulse was to protest, to say that I wasn't feeling well. I was tired of running errands, but I had tried this trick in the past and it didn't work. Grandma always looked suspicious and most likely would tell me I was lying.

Minutes later I was on my way. I was about halfway over the first hill when I began feeling very weak. I thought I was overcome by the heat because I was sweating profusely. I had developed a terrible headache, and I could hardly keep the basket on my head. Each step I made seemed to increase the severity and frequency of the pain, and I kept swaying and staggering.

By the grace of God, I managed to make my way to Aunt Lulu's home. She realized right away that something was wrong with me. I was weak and shaking so violently that I could hardly stand up. Aunt Lulu took one look at me and without saying a word carried me to a bed. Soon I had an attack of some sort and heard an unbearable noise in my head. I couldn't take the pain and noise anymore. "There is too much noise," I remember saying over and over.

It didn't help that Aunt Lulu kept assuring me, "No one is saying a word, there is no noise."

Moments later I was overcome by such an agonizing headache and overpowering noise inside my head that I did not know where I was, and then, mercifully, I didn't know anything anymore.

CHAPTER 2

The Sound of Silence

T
HE NEXT THING I knew, someone in a white coat was bending over me. My whole body hurt, and I could barely breathe or move. Somewhere in the room I heard a voice saying, "She is back."

I looked around. I was in a strange room, a strange bed, with railings on all four sides. I didn't know what had happened to me, or how I had gotten there. I had this strange feelings that I had been in another place, just before I opened my eyes a place where I felt no pain. I remember seeing a beautiful gate with thousands of lights of every colors. I wished I could go back to that beautiful, calm, and peaceful place and stay there forever.

I had never been to a hospital before, and it took me some time to realize that I was isolated in a hospital room. The only visitors I had were the doctor and the nurses, who came in every now and then to check on me, change my clothes, and give me medication. As my condition improved, I began to observe everything around me. I felt isolated and scared, being alone in a room by myself. I kept watching the door, hoping that my father or some other family member would come to get me. It might have been only a few weeks but it felt like months before my father came to see me. I had definitely given up hope of ever seeing my family again, but then one day the door opened, and I caught a glimpse of Dad and his friend Zeke. Dad was walking behind the nurse, a head taller than her.

The unexpected sight of my father suddenly gave me the strength to spring shakily to my feet, holding on to the bed railing for support. I don't know how I managed to stand up, because I couldn't even sit up. My hope was that Dad had come to get me out of the hospital. His visit was brief, though, and when I realized that he was leaving without me, I held tightly to his shirt, begging and pleading, "Take me home, Dad, take me with you," I screamed as Dad, with the help of his friend Zeke, pried open my fingers. After Dad left, I fell asleep, exhausted, with the echo of my screams still ringing in my ears.

I didn't see my father or any of my relatives for a long time after this, and I despaired of ever getting out of the hospital. I had been there for so long. My biggest fear was that I would never see my family or my home again.

I felt relieved when the nurse moved me into another ward, where there were about a dozen children. Unfortunately, I am unable to recall hearing anything then. Not long afterward, my father came to see me. My heart was pounding as he held up one of my school dresses and lifted me in his arms. I said, "I am going home with you, Dad! I am going back to school!"

When the nurse took off the hospital robe that I had been wearing for so long and pulled my dress over my head, I was overjoyed. I knew I was going home at last! I ran through the aisle between the rows of beds in the hospital ward, just to show Dad that I was well enough to go home.

During the ride home, I thought of nothing else but seeing my family and friends again. I was still very sick, and I became tired during the long ride, but I was afraid to close my eyes. I was afraid that I'd fall asleep and wake up to find myself back in the hospital. As we passed my school, I just couldn't contain my excitement. I clapped my hands and exclaimed, "Look, Dad, there is my school! I am going to school tomorrow." I can't recall what my father said, or if he said anything at all. But then, I didn't expect an answer, and it didn't matter to me. All that mattered was that I was going home.

Despite my excitement and my fears, I fell asleep. I woke up to find a hand lifting me and carrying me into our home. A few of my relatives were in the living room.

What stands out most in my memory is how strange it seemed, that everyone was greeting me in silence. There wasn't a sound anywhere in the room, but then I had been confined to a hospital bed for so long, I might have gotten used to the silence. One by one, my relatives came forward to hug and greet me. I immediately sensed something was wrong when I realized that their lips were moving but not a sound was coming from any of them. Grandma was bending over me, her lips moving, I tried to make sense of what she was saying, but I didn't hear anything.

In the weeks that followed I remained confined to my bed, unable to keep my balance. Perhaps I was too sick to notice how quiet the home had became, but after a time I became very perplexed. The lack of sounds everywhere was beginning to bother me. My family's voices were as familiar to me as their faces, and I fully expected to hear their voices as well as seeing their faces. Though I had been in the hospital for three months, I never believed I had been there. I had a strange feeling that the hospital experience was just a bad dream.

For months I remained weak and delirious from all the medications I was taking. I slept most of the time and stayed in bed even when awake, barely aware of what was going on around me and annoyed that I couldn't walk straight. I had constant headaches, and the constant ringing in my ears was unbearable.

Although I was not aware of it then, I was later convinced that my hearing had been deteriorating over a period of time. Every now and then, I could hear a voice, but I couldn't make out what was being said. I noticed that no one seemed to call my name anymore, and I couldn't understand why everyone had began touching me to get my attention.

It took several months before I felt well enough to go outside for a walk. I remember standing outside the barbed wire fence and looking out at the farm, thrilled to feel the cool air blowing gently at my face. As I walked along, I looked around. Everything was strangely calm and peaceful: The cows were grazing in the field. The horse was in the stable. I made my way toward the sprawling shade tree where I loved to watch and listen to the birds. As I settled on the soft grass I saw several birds perched on the branches. They were opening and closing their beaks just as they always did when they were singing. I lay in the grass for a long time, staring up at the birds, waiting for the familiar sounds that never came. Disappointed, I walked away, our two dogs trotting alongside me. I couldn't hear their playful barking. Everything seemed so unreal. I tried to dismiss it, but I couldn't escape the stark reality. Perhaps something else was taking place in my mind, something I didn't recognize because I had never experienced anything like it before. I believe that God was protecting me from the unbearable, painful loss that I was about to experience.

Despite the glimmers of awareness, I received a shock some days later. Two of my playmates invited me to go outside to play hide-and-seek with them. It was pitch dark as I walked outside. I stood in the darkness swaying, feeling unbalanced and more confused than ever. As I tried to focus on the two shadowy figures, I realized that I couldn't see or hear them. The knowledge that I could no longer hear was beginning to creep in on me. I'd never felt so lost and helpless in my life. Standing alone in the silent darkness, I felt like I had lost both senses, hearing and sight.

Frightened, confused, and emotionally upset, I ran back into the house and collapsed on the bed. Moments later I saw my playmates coming toward me, but I pulled the pillow over my head and tried to stifle my sobs. I didn't want to talk to any of them. I didn't want them to feel sorry for me.

Nothing was the same for me after that. I became sensitive to the way my playmates spoke to me. At first I thought they were just playing whispering games with me. In fact, we used to play whispering games to each other before I lost my hearing. I became annoyed at the constant touching and gesturing and having to guess what they were saying. One day I was sitting outside with a group of my cousins. When one of them threw a ball to get my attention, I was pretty upset.

"Stop throwing things at me," I shouted, ready to pick a fight, but I heard nothing.

But they were all laughing. "We were shouting your name and you didn't hear." There were times when I could still hear some words, but my playmates thought I could still hear them if they shouted.

When I shouted back at them, I realized that no matter how loudly I shouted, I could not hear my own voice or my friends' voices. Then they began telling me constantly. "Speak a little louder" or "I can't hear a word you say." At first, I thought there was a problem with my voice, and I felt helpless with the realization that I could no longer monitor my own voice—a voice I could no longer hear.

This was a time of great stress for me, knowing that all my playmates were going to school. I desperately wanted to go back to school. I can't count the number of times Grandma promised, "Next week you can go with Doris or Angela," but next week never came. Worse, I was no longer allowed to go anywhere, even with friends. Grandma had stopped taking me with her to church or to visit relatives. It broke my heart that she took Audley and Val everywhere with her and left me home.

My life had changed drastically. I continued to interact with my playmates, but I no longer played games on the farm with them. By communicating with my playmates, I was actually learning lipreading without even knowing it.

As I look back on this stage of my life, it is a challenge to separate facts from fantasy. I was still in denial then, unable to accept the fact that I could no longer hear. It was a miracle that I was able to understand my hearing friends. I think my lipreading ability was a natural transition, a gift from God that enabled me to shift from hearing words to seeing words. I call this ability to lip-read "developing a hearing vision."

In those days, I fantasized that one day my hearing would return as mysteriously as it had disappeared. One day, as I lay on the cool grass, looking up at the caves, I remembered the wonderful times my playmates and I had enjoyed playing there. I remembered the thrill of hearing the echo of my voice. I got up and yelled, "Hello!" to the caves. I stood there waiting, willing myself to hear the echo. But there was nothing but silence. Even my voice didn't seem to work anymore. I placed my hands around my neck and yelled, "Hello!" again and again. I could feel the vibration in my neck. Somehow I knew that I wasn't hearing my own voice, yet something inside me just couldn't admit that I was unable to hear anything. I think something in my mind was blocking the truth to protect me from the unbearable pain of recognizing the loss.

I lived in this state of mind for several months. Books became my constant companions, my escape from a world of silence. I read anything I could find in the home. Luckily, my three months in school had helped me to build a solid foundation for words. My reading ability improved as I read more books and magazines. Soon I had developed such a passion for books that I was sure I couldn't survive without a book to read. I had read all the fairy-tale books and magazines I could get my hands on and began reading history books. I borrowed books from my playmates. Everything I read was fascinating to me, and I never read a book I didn't like.

Up to this time, the Bible was the only book in the house I hadn't bothered to read. I remember leafing through its pages one day and finding it full of names that I couldn't pronounce. It was such a big book, and I didn't know where to look for the answers to the many questions that filled my mind. I was always aware that there was a Supreme Being watching over us. My idea of God was a big loving person who would not allow anything bad to happen to those He loved. I had always believed that sickness, accidents, and death were the works of the devil.

"If God loves me," I said to Dad one day, "why did He allow the devil to take away my hearing?"

Dad sat there looking at me, puzzled. Finally he said, "God would never allow the devil to touch you." He went on to explain that "all sickness came from God."

"Are you saying God allowed this to happen to me?" I cried. "He has no love for me."

I felt as if I had been punched in the stomach. Knowing that my hearing loss and illness came from God was hard for me to accept. I could never think of a loving God putting a curse on someone, and to me, deafness was a curse. From that day, I began to rebel against God.

I didn't realize at the time that my passion for books was rapidly improving my reading and writing. By reading so many books, I was able to keep up with my playmates, who were going to school regularly. Unfortunately, it was not until some years later that I realized that many of the words I had learned from reading books were spelled one way but pronounced another. I had added many words to my vocabulary visually—from reading books. I only became aware that I had a problem pronouncing some of the words when I began using them in my speech. I then became aware that teaching myself to pronounce some words without hearing them was not going to be easy. Yet I was happy with what I had achieved. I had come a long way in teaching myself to read and write.

One of my biggest discoveries around this time was how easy it was for me to read my own lips. It happened one day as I was arranging my hair in the mirror. I was repeating a poem I had just read, and as I watched the movements of my lips in the mirror, I realized that I could make out every word I was saying. Talking to myself in the mirror became a fascinating game! I'd whisper so that no none could hear me, but I quickly learned some simple tricks. Soon I was a pro at guessing words. I made a game of guessing the missing words in a sentence, and I encouraged all my friends to speak to me in their normal voices. It was frustrating when family members began repeating one word at a time, thinking it was easier for me to follow. But it was difficult for me. By the time I had guessed the last word, the whole meaning of the sentence was lost. I let my family understand that it was easier for me to follow their normal speech in a conversation.

I saw very little of my father during this time, so I was very happy when he took me out one day for a ride on his bike. After months of being confined to the house with nowhere to go, it was refreshing to be going somewhere.

I didn't know where we were going, but I didn't care. We rode on and on, until Dad turned the bike into a narrow dirt road, and we got off in front of a little red house. Taking me by the hand, he said, "We are going inside to see a very nice lady who can help you."

My curiosity got the better of me, and I couldn't help asking, "Who is she, Dad? What is she going to do?"

Dad looked sad. "She will pray for you," he said after a long pause. "Just sit and be quiet."

The interior of the house was very dark with only one shuttered window, and I was overcome by a strong smell. We were greeted by a strange woman who wore a bold-patterned, tent-shaped dress, with a matching scarf tied around her head.

"Mother Anne will make you well again. Go with her," Dad told me as the woman came forward and took my hand. She led me into a strange room and let go of my hand. I watched as she arranged a chair and stood with her eyes closed and her hands clasped together in prayer. I stood in the center of the room, staring at the lighted candles and the strange drawings on the wall. When she opened her eyes, she motioned for me to come forward and sit in the chair. I did. She placed both her hands on my head, then stood staring at something as if she was in a trance. Then, as we left, she gave Dad two little bottles of something, which I later learned was frankincense and myrrh.

Grandma poured some of the contents of those bottles onto my head each day. I hated the smell. It was gummy and sticky, and it glued my hair to my scalp, making it impossible to comb my hair.

A million questions raced through my mind: *Why are they doing all this to me? Why are they putting me through all these strange rituals?* These were questions I couldn't answer, but subconsciously I knew that they were hoping that my hearing would be restored through spiritual means. But after only one session with Mother Anne, Dad just gave up.

I became sensitive to the fact that I was being treated differently when we had visitors. Audley was one year younger than I was and he was always encouraged to talk to our guests, but I was always discouraged from talking to any of them. If any of our guests tried to say something to me, someone would always step in and interrupt by saying, "She can't hear you know." If I said something, a family member would step in and interrupt, asking, "What were you trying to say, dear?"

"Don't talk to people," Grandma lectured me. "Your voice is not the same, and no one will understand you."

I remember one day when Grandma's sister, Aunt Gee, was visiting with her daughter Muriel. Muriel was about my age, and looked friendly. I wanted to talk to her, but I was afraid she wouldn't understand me. After constantly being told that no one could understand me I had became self-conscious about my voice. I had become too timid to approach anyone. But as soon as I had the opportunity I said to Grandma, "Can I talk to Muriel?"

"I don't know if she can understand you, but you can talk to her," Grandma replied.

Muriel and I became the best of friends, a friendship that lasted until the day of her death.

More than anything in the world, I hated being pitied, especially by visiting relatives who would pat me on the head and say, "Poor little thing."

Although I was bombarded on every side with evidence that I could no longer hear, I was still in denial about my hearing loss. One day, I was playing with a string of beads when the thread suddenly snapped, scattering the beads all over the floor. Ever mindful of the fact that Aunt Vie could easily trip over them since she couldn't see them, I ran into the kitchen to get something to store the beads. I stood on my tiptoes, trying to reach an empty jam jar on the top shelf. The jar tipped over sideways and began rolling toward the end of the shelf. I knew it was going to crash, but it was out of my reach. Automatically, I put my hands over my ears, fully expecting to hear the crashing sounds of broken glass. Instead, I felt a thump, and then a shock went through me. The jar fell to the floor, breaking as silently as paper into splintered pieces. Before I knew it, everyone was by my side, wanting to know what had happened. I knew immediately that they had heard the crashing sounds of the broken jar. I sat down heavily on a nearby bench, wondering why I hadn't heard the crash.

Everyone was asking, "Did you hear it?"

I couldn't answer. I just stared at the broken jar until the tears blurred my eyes. Over and over, the tormenting question repeated itself in my mind: *Why didn't I hear the bottle as it crashed to the floor?* It was like the end of the world for me.

It was out of sheer loneliness and frustration, I suppose, that I made my first doll from some scraps of cloth I found in the house. Pretty soon I had six rag dolls. Two of them were more beautiful than the others, so I dressed them in all the prettiest dresses I made. I improved these two dolls by adding eyes, a mouth, and a nose with embroidery thread. I made their hair from the stalks of young corn. To me they looked blonde and beautiful. I was proud of my two dolls and spent a lot of time dressing them. Their names were Marlin and Elizabeth.

When I wasn't playing with my dolls or making doll dresses, I was in a fantasy world with a book. With books, I could forget myself and what I had become; I began living vicariously through books. My playmates had, by then, become sensitive to my needs—instead of calling to me, they would tap me on the shoulder and come around to face me when they spoke. I had perfected my lipreading ability by this time. I also managed to learn a lot by watching the facial expressions of my friends and relatives.

I could always tell from facial expression when they were talking too loud. When said something exciting. When they were whispering, or when they spoke angry or sad.

It was more than a year after I had been out of the hospital that Audley started going to school. To make matters worse, some of the neighbor children began dropping by on their way to school. I desperately wanted to go back to school. Every day, I sat outside on the doorsteps and cried as I watched the other children go off to school.

Once Grandma had dressed Audley and sent him off to school, she would go off to her gardening job and leave me and my four-year-old brother, Val, in the care of Aunt Vie. Aunt Vie couldn't do much for us, and I was bored staying inside the house all day. As soon as Grandma was out of the house, I would grab a pillow and a book and head for a shady tree on the farm. I would sit there and read; soon I would be absorbed in the book, my mind a million miles away from all my problems. Books, became my constant companions, my escape from a world of heartbreak.

The final blow to my fantasy world came one morning as I watched Audley and some of my playmates getting ready to leave for school. That morning, Grandma had handed me a neatly ironed dress and had combed my hair. I got the impression that I was going to school with the other children. Without thinking, I ran to get my book and pencil. I was out of the house before I knew it, running toward the front gate. Suddenly I felt a hand grab me from behind. I looked up into Grandma's face, and I couldn't help noticing that she was crying. As she took my hand and led me back to the house, I saw Aunt Vie standing outside, and she was also crying. In that instant, I understood my situation. Remembered scenes from the day I came back from the hospital played over and over in my mind. I looked over at Grandma and Aunt Vie, and I knew why they were both crying. Everything that had happened to me in the past year came rushing back to me, and with it came the awful realization that I was never going back to school because I was deaf. I thought of all the years that I had refused to accept the fact that I could no longer hear. I had been living in a make-believe world to escape the real world with all the pain and heartbreak of accepting my hearing loss.

As I watched Grandma and Aunt Vie crying, I suddenly knew what I had to do. I wanted to tell them how sorry I was. I knew they were crying for me, for the fact that I was never going back to school. The unspoken words between us were that no one in the family had ever said that I was deaf, and I had never accepted that fact. Suddenly I wanted to comfort

Grandma and Aunt Vie. I wanted them to know it wasn't their fault why I was not going back to school. I wanted them to know that I understood.

Slowly, I walked up to Grandma. Putting my hands on her shoulder, I said, "Grandma, please don't cry." I went on. "It's not your fault that I am not going to school; I know why I am not going back. I don't want you to cry for me. It's because …" but I couldn't say the words. After what seemed like an eternity, I found the courage to say the three most heartbreaking words for the first time in my life. "I am deaf."

Suddenly I was running from the house, running, from the awful reality of what my life had become. I was sobbing uncontrollably as Grandma reached out to me and led me back to the house.

After this heartrending admission, I was plunged into a deep depression. I didn't want to think. I didn't want to feel. In fact, I didn't want to exist at all. I lost interest in everything and refused to go outside and play. Everything around the home became a constant reminder that I could no longer hear. My playmates, the cat and dogs, the birds, even the wind in the trees.

I must have continued in this listless existence for a couple of weeks. One day, I happened to glance in the mirror and was shocked at my appearance. I couldn't believe what I saw. My hair was matted and glued to my scalp from the perpetual use of the frankincense and myrrh. My body was thin and skinny. Looking at myself, I was filled with both sorrow and self-pity. I hadn't realized how much the emotional torment of the past weeks had worn me down, but I knew I couldn't go on living like this. If I wanted to go on living, I knew I had to do something.

It took extraordinary courage and incredible willpower to accept myself as I was. I decided I had to do something about my appearance. I bathed and washed my hair, carefully removing all traces of the gum. After a week or so, I was pleased with my clean-cut appearance, but I couldn't get over the feelings of self-pity and emotional turmoil that had become a part of my daily life. Once again I turned to books to help me forget. *The Sleeping Beauty* and *Westward Ho*, for example, were books that really helped to break through my extreme depression. I wanted to forget everything about my hearing loss so badly that I buried myself in books. I read so many books that I was almost living in another world, a world that, at times, seemed more real than anything around me.

One day when I was outside playing with my two best dolls, I came across two of the other dolls that I had discarded because they weren't pretty enough. Suddenly I felt sick. I felt like the discarded dolls in God's eyes. I felt ugly and rejected. Once again, I turned to books to help me forget.

After more than a year of rebellion, I was convinced that God would never forgive me. I had read somewhere that all manner of sin and blasphemy shall be forgiven unto men, but the blasphemy against the Holy Ghost shall not be forgiven unto men. This verse from Matthew 12:31 sent a shudder running through me. I felt I was condemned to everlasting punishment, that there was no hope for me. In desperation I began reading the Bible, searching for something that would give me hope.

One day some evangelists came to our home. They gave me a pocket-sized New Testament and a little booklet. The booklet held the answers to many of the questions in my mind. I decided to read the Bible from Genesis to Revelation. It took me several months to complete my reading of the Bible, but I came away convinced that God had forgiven me. For the first time in my life, I was blissfully happy.

Reading the Bible and praying every day had now became a part of my life. I felt a deep sense of inner peace. I had faith in God and a feeling of hope I had never experienced before with books. With books I could forget myself and what I was, but meditating and praying to God brought me peace of mind. With books I had to live in a fantasy world to forget my problems. With faith I could accept myself as I was and be content with my lot.

I began to feel that God had a purpose for me, that He wanted me to do something with my life. From that day on I was at peace. I think a protective barrier had formed around my heart, making the pain easier to bear.

CHAPTER 3

A Ray of Hope

SEVERAL WEEKS AFTER I had accepted my unhappy fate, I went back to my old school for a visit, accompanied by my half-sister, Esmie, my father's fifteen-year-old daughter. As we neared the school, I could see many of my playmates playing outside with some of my school friends. I realized it was recess time. Fear gripped me, and I suddenly became acutely aware of my hearing loss. *How would my school friends react when they saw me?* I wondered. *Would any of them come forward to greet me? Would any of them want to be my friend again?* Suddenly I turned to Esmie.

"Please, let's go home," I begged. "I don't want go any farther. I don't want the children to see me."

She looked at me, shocked. "Why?" she asked. "You have always wanted to go back to school."

"Not anymore," I said. "No one is going to like me. I want to go home."

She looked confused. "Well," she said, "if you don't want the children to see you, then you'd better hurry before the bell rings."

I walked as fast as I could, thankful that no one recognized us as we made our way up those familiar stairs, in the place that had once brought me so much happiness.

All the teachers seemed surprised and happy to see me. Teacher Henry, who was the headmaster, lifted me up and placed me on his lap. He was saying something to me when suddenly I was aware that a crowd had gathered around us. I looked up into a sea of faces. Hundreds of eyes were staring at me. All of a sudden, the school was filled with children, pushing and shoving each other to get a better view of me. The teachers tried in vain to bring order. I fought back tears, knowing that I was the reason for all the commotion.

As we left the school, I knew it was the end of my hopes and dreams of going back to school. As we walked home, I remembered a conversation with my father.

He had told me, "Nita, I can't send you back to school. You can't hear, and children will make fun of you."

"Dad," I had asked, "will I be able to hear again someday?"

"I am praying for you," he had said, "God has a plan for you."

One day I asked, "Dad, if I pray to God, will He hear me?"

"I am sure he will hear you, child," he said.

From that day, I had started to pray every night. "Now I lay me down to sleep, Heavenly Father, hear my cry," and then I had added, "Lord, help me to hear again so that I can go back to school; Lord, help me to hear again so that others will not make fun of me." I prayed every night for several weeks but became very discouraged when nothing seemed to happen.

Then, one day I sat outside making a paper hat. As I pulled the funnel-shaped hat over my ears, I heard a loud cracking noise in my left ear. I patted the paper again and again, just to make sure I wasn't imagining things. Excitedly, I ran into the kitchen looking for Grandma. She was sitting on a bench, shelling some peas.

"Grandma," I said, touching my left ear. "I heard this paper making a loud noise in this ear!"

She didn't seem surprised. Without looking up she asked, "Are you sure you heard the paper?"

"Yes!" I said smiling. "It was loud and clear."

"Turn around," she said. "Close your eyes."

I turned around and closed my eyes. Nothing happened. When I opened my eyes, Grandma was in front of me.

"Did you hear me call you?"

"No," I admitted.

"Well," Grandma said, "you did not hear the paper, you must have felt the paper against your ears."

But I had many reasons to believe that I had some hearing in my left ear. Every time I took a bath and heard the popping noise of the soapsuds in my left ear, I had reason to hope. I also discovered that if my playmates shouted in my left ear, I could hear their voices. These and other sounds around the home gave me hope.

My biggest hope was that my father would take me to see an ear specialist. But my father insisted that there was no doctor in the world who could restore hearing. "Only God can do that," he said.

Around this time, I saw an ad for hearing aids in a magazine. The ad convinced me that a hearing aid would work for me. One ad stated that the hearing aid was a miraculous new invention, so powerful that it could make anyone who was deaf "hear a pin drop." I figured that, if I could hear the cracking sounds of paper, soapsuds, and other sounds, then I should be able to hear with a hearing aid. I knew many people who wore eyeglasses because they couldn't read without them. I figured that hearing aids would work somewhat like eyeglasses, you just put them on and you hear.

Although my family never said anything about taking me to a doctor, much less a specialist, I kept hoping that one day my father would change his mind and take me to get my hearing tested. I still had earaches and occasional swellings in both ears that were so painful, I had to lie down with cold pads pressed against each ear.

Knowing that there were doctors who specialized in hearing loss, I refused to give up hope. Dr. Johnson, the doctor who saved my life at Black River Hospital, was not an ear specialist. He had no experience with hearing loss. He didn't know what had caused my illness, and he didn't know how, or why, I had lost my hearing.

As far as I knew, Dr. Johnson was the only doctor serving several districts where we lived. His most important mission was saving lives. Very few people in the 1940s went to doctors for checkups. I had never been to a doctor before my sudden illness, and I never went back for a checkup after I left the hospital.

After more than two years of living in silence, my biggest concern was having to grow up in a world geared for the hearing. I couldn't understand why Dad and Grandma did everything they could to discourage me. I wasn't allowed to talk about seeing a specialist, and after a time it became a forbidden topic in our family.

I was almost ten years old when I stopped playing with dolls and making dolls' dresses. Grandma had told me that I could have my mother's sewing machine, since no one was using it. I had always wanted to make a dress of my own, but I had no material. One day, as I was sorting through some discarded clothes that Grandma had bundled together and kept under her bed, I came across a beautiful floral dress that had once belonged to Aunt Vie. Aunt Vie had put on some weight, and the dress no longer fit her.

I will never forget the day I got a pair of scissors and started cutting the material. It felt wonderful in my hands. From the material, I made myself a very simple dress with a square neckline, a full-flared skirt, and a few tiny buttons all the way to the hem. When the dress was finished, I couldn't believe I had made it. It looked so beautiful, I was almost afraid to try it on. I stood before a full-length mirror. To my surprise, the dress fit perfectly! I wanted to dance and sing. I felt like Cinderella as I wheeled around the floor. This was the first time I had made a real dress (instead of dolls' dresses), and it was an exhilarating new experience for me. I realized that I could do a lot of things my hearing friends were not doing. I vowed I would do everything possible to make my family realize that life for me wasn't over just because I couldn't hear anymore. I realized I could make beautiful dresses for myself, instead of the plain chambray dresses I was accustomed to wearing.

Throughout my tenth birthday, I kept hoping for a miracle. But I realized that I had no choice but to accept my hearing loss with grace and dignity. Deafness, however, was not the biggest obstacle in my life at this stage. It was the painful reactions of my family and friends that made life an emotionally draining experience for me.

At this stage, I had came to accept the fact that my voice was changing— but then, there was nothing I could do. Since I could no longer hear my own voice, I tried to speak the way I was accustomed to speaking before I lost my hearing. It was disappointing when concerned family and friends began asking, "What's wrong with your voice?"

I helplessly shrugged my shoulders, because I didn't even know what my voice sounded like anymore. I had no way of knowing when there was background noise. For instance. in my hearing days, I could adjust my voice to the varying degrees of sounds going on around me without thinking. Whenever I became conscious that there was something wrong, I did my best to adjust and speak as normally as possible by concentrating on the way I used to speak during my hearing days. I knew I was fighting a losing battle, though, when my friends began making comments such as, "You must be getting a bad cold."

Other times, I thought I was speaking normally, only to be asked. "Why are you whispering?" If I raised my voice a little, the comment always was, "Now you are speaking too loudly." Eventually, I learned to keep my voice at a comfortable pitch by carefully watching the reactions of others when I was speaking to them.

Since I was unable to hear the voices of my friends when we were in a group, I would just sit and watch them as they talked. I longed for the days when I was able to enjoy easy, relaxing communication with friends without gazing into their faces. I had gotten pretty good at lip-reading, but I didn't realize that I was missing so many words. My friends laughed at how I got my words mixed up. I soon saw how funny it was and learned to laugh along with them.

To my dismay, I soon found out that many words looked alike when people spoke them, especially names and places. I couldn't tell the difference between Mummy and Bobby, for example. As I got older, I learned to look for other cues. It was like guessing a couple of words crossed out in a sentence. I was young, and I had a lot to learn. I learned about facial expressions and body language, which offered some of the biggest cues to guessing the words that were invisible on people's lips.

I was disturbed by my family's decision to shield me from visitors to our home. I felt incomplete. Unlike the other children, I wasn't supposed to speak to anyone except close family members.

So I was pleasantly surprised one day when Grandma beckoned me into the kitchen where she was preparing lunch. "We are having visitors," she announced. "Go and take a bath, I will bring you a dress." I bathed and dressed quickly, wondering who I was going to meet. I was nervous at the thought of meeting visitors and being told they were not going to understand me.

The moment I walked into the kitchen, Grandma said, "Get out the knives and forks, and set the table."

"Who is coming?" I wanted to know.

"Your Aunt Doris and her daughters."

While I set the table, my mind raced around trying to picture what Aunt Doris's daughters looked like. I had met Aunt Doris several times, and she was always immaculately dressed, but I had never met any of her daughters. I was told they were city girls going to a college in Kingston, and I was eager to meet them.

I was just about to put the finishing touches on the table when there was a tap on my shoulder. I looked around to see Grandma's sister, Aunt Doris. Behind her stood three beautiful girls looking as if they had just stepped out of the pages of an expensive fashion magazine. Aunt Doris's daughters, Emery, Margaret, and Lynn, made such a big impression on me that from that day, I copied every dress that resembled what they were wearing. I told myself that when I grew up, I was going to sew some of the most beautiful dresses for myself. I wanted desperately to look and dress like my cousins—beautiful, sophisticated, and educated.

I found myself living in an imaginary world where only good things would happen to me. Even though I was aware that my fantasy world was unreal, it was better than living in a heartbreaking world without a future.

Once I had given up hope of going back to school. I began studying all of Audley's books and any other books I could get my hands on. I saw education as the only road to success. My family couldn't understand why I was so obsessed with books or why I wanted so badly to have a good education, and they did their best to stop me from reading books.

When Audley was off to school and the rest of the family was busy on the farm, I stayed in my favorite hiding place. I was so preoccupied with my hearing loss and my own needs that I hadn't noticed how lonely my five-year-old brother was. I didn't realize how much Val needed me until I found him wandering around the farm one day, looking for me. He was crying. I dropped the book I was reading and got to my feet as fast as I could. I ran toward him, calling his name.

As I picked him up and held him close to me, I could feel the beating of his heart against my chest. He buried his little face close to my ear and cried. With a mixture of both sadness and relief, I listened to his cries. I was sad that I had not heard his voice since he was two years old, but I also felt a sense of relief that at least I could hear something. It gave me hope. I held my little brother for a long time, until he fell asleep, and then I carried him back to the house.

"Where have you been?" Aunt Vie asked as I came through the door. Although she couldn't see us, I know she recognized my footsteps. "I kept calling for Val," she said. "When he didn't answer I didn't know what to do." I saw the worried look on her face.

"There was nothing else you could do," I assured her. "He is here with me. He is asleep." Suddenly I knew it was true. She couldn't do much to help. She might have heard Val crying, but she couldn't see where he was going. I walked over to the corner and laid my little brother on the bed, then stood for a moment, watching the rise and fall of his chest. He was sleeping so peacefully, and then I realized how much he had grown. I felt guilty. I had missed out on so much of his growing years because I had been so wrapped up in my own little world.

"Why can't you stay inside?" Aunt Vie asked. "Your brother is always running outside looking for you every day."

Suddenly I was overcome by a burst of emotion. I realized how complicated life was for the three of us: Aunt Vie, myself, and my little brother. I knew that Aunt Vie was unable to find her way outside the house without a guide, and I couldn't hear my brother calling for me. For the first time, I felt the pain of loneliness and frustration that my mother was dead and my father was not there for us.

Grandma became annoyed that I was reading so many books and spending most of my time outside. "Why are you reading so many books?" she demanded. "You know it's a waste of time."

I looked into Grandma's serious gray eyes, and knew she really meant it. "What about Audley?" I found myself saying. "You are always encouraging him to study, and getting him books to read."

"Audley is going to school. He needs to study. Books are for people who are going to school," She went on. "You are not going to school, and you don't need to study, so there is no need for you to read any books."

By now I was close to tears, but I tried not to show it. I hoped Grandma would understand that I had the same hopes and dreams as anyone else. Instead I said innocently, "These books I am reading are helping me to learn what all my friends are learning in school."

"You can't teach yourself," Grandma said seriously. "You would be better off doing something constructive like sewing."

I should have seen it coming but I was still surprised when Grandma decided that it was time for me to take on some of the housework. "From now on," she told me one morning, "your job is to make the beds, sweep, clean, and polish the floor. No more reading books and idleness." She went on to say that every Monday morning I would have to help with the family laundry. Doing the family laundry was difficult for me. They were farmers' clothes, made from thick khaki fabric, very dirty and hard to clean. Worst yet, they had to be scrubbed by hands. The first time I did the laundry I had pain in my wrist for a month. Since I wanted so much to be treated like I was part of the family, I didn't mind helping as long as

I was also allowed to read and study with any of my playmates who were available.

Around this time I began to think of telling my story, since my life was so unusual, complicated, and different from all the other children I knew. I felt that telling my story was the only way I could get my family to see me as a person. Inspired by a story I once read, I felt my true light was hidden from the world. So one day I sat down and wrote a two-page story. I poured out all the frustration and loneliness I felt. I wanted my family to understand what hearing loss was like. I wanted them to understand the devastating impact it had on my life. But more than anything else, I wanted them to understand that I was determined to live my life as normally as possible.

I had forgotten all about the story I had written until one day my cousin read it. He began to cry. "You have such a wonderful intelligence," he said. "You could even write a book."

When we had important visiting relatives, our family's custom was to stand outside our home waiting to greet our guests. I would often stand in line just like the others, waiting for a handshake. I was always troubled when our guests would go around shaking the hands of everyone, but look right over me as though I didn't exist. I now understand why so many of our relatives acted that way. I have realized that it is easy for many hearing people to overlook someone who can't hear. They don't realize that a nod or a gesture is all it takes to make someone who can't hear happy. I don't think that people in these situations are aware that their behavior is hurtful; after all, most of them have never have never given deafness a second thought.

On my tenth birthday, Grandma took me with her to visit Aunt Lulu, who had given birth to a baby girl (who she named Jessie) ten days before. I was overjoyed when she told me to wear the dress I had made for myself the month before. Many of our neighbors had assembled at Aunt Lulu's house to welcome her new baby, and it seemed that everyone who was there wanted to know who had made the dress I was wearing. I didn't know it then, but my life was about to change dramatically.

A couple of weeks later, Grandma and I were sitting in the kitchen shelling some peas when one of our neighbors came visiting. She smiled and patted me on the head, then walked over and took a seat next to Grandma. I continued shelling the peas while she chatted with Grandma, keeping my eyes on their faces. I was curious to know what they were talking about. I soon realized they were talking about me.

"That child is very talented," Alice was saying. "How did she learn to sew that dress she made for herself?"

"You'd be surprised," Grandma said laughing. "She's been sewing dolls' clothes for more than a year." She continued, "I can't keep a scrap of cloth around here."

I blushed as they both looked at me, but I said nothing. I didn't want them to know I was observing what they were saying.

The next thing I knew, Alice was asking Grandma for permission to let me sew some dresses for her four children.

"Well," Grandma said to me later that day, "I am happy for you. You finally have a job. Sewing kids' clothes will keep you from going crazy with books."

I didn't know what to say, so Grandma went on talking. "You don't need books or education. You should be happy you have a job. How many ten-year-olds can sew like you?"

I started to protest but Grandma cut me off. "Alice promised to show off the dresses you are going to sew for her children." She went on, " Nita, do you realize that many of the neighbors would like you to make dresses for their kids?"

It was a wonderful turning point in my life, and it couldn't have happened at a better time. Ready-to-wear clothes in Jamaica were very expensive, at that time, and few people could afford them. Most families owned a sewing machine, and would try to sew clothing for themselves and their families, often with unsatisfactory results.

My success as a child seamstress depended a great deal on luck, as well as a lot of hard work and practice. I didn't have any fashion magazines, so I collected clippings from magazines and newspapers. By stapling them together, I assembled a collection of different styles, but I soon found out that most of the mothers wanted something exclusive for their children. My first attempt at sketching came when one of the parents came to me and said, "I am taking my daughter to church next Sunday. Could you design something special for her?" Two days later, I showed her a sketch I had made especially for her. She loved it, and I was able make her daughter's dress from the sketch.

Pretty soon, many local families sought me out for special designs. I did my best to make sure that no two children were dressed alike for special occasions. Fortunately, most of the parents wanted a design like a dress I had made before.

Designing and sewing dresses for kids brought me unexpected success. I had great fun dressing up the local girls. To me, they were all beautiful living dolls, and they came to love me as much as I loved them. One day, a group of girls were passing my home. The moment they saw me, they began shouting excitedly, "Nita, Nita." Although I couldn't hear them, I could tell by their pretty little faces bursting with happiness that they were very glad to see me. On one such occasions, I just couldn't stand where I was. I walked over to them and hugged each one. Those wonderful kids gave me so much happiness.

CHAPTER 4

The Little Seamstress

W HEN I BEGAN sewing children clothes, I wasn't sewing for the money; I simply loved to sew. For me, sewing was a hobby, something I really enjoyed doing. Best of all, it was good to know I was doing something important to help others and getting respect in return. My neighbors paid me what they wanted, or what they could afford. At this time, having communication with many of my neighbors was helping me to feel more confident. I soon became known as the little seamstress.

Because I was earning a little money, I made a little drawstring bag and began saving. I was still collecting magazines that advertised hearing aids. I hoped to earn and save enough money to pay for a hearing evaluation and possibly a hearing aid. What really gave me hope was the fact that I still could hear some sounds in my left ear. Unfortunately, my family remained strictly opposed to any suggestion I made concerning medical attention. I could never understand why they refused to take me to have my hearing evaluated. They made it plain that no doctor could help me because I didn't have enough hearing, but I did not believe them.

At any rate, I decided to keep my intentions a secret. I told myself that one day I would get all the medical help I needed, and I began to save all my money. Still, I had no idea how I would go about getting medical help. I was too young to do anything on my own, and I was desperate to go back to school. I was aware that my hearing loss was the main reason why I was not going to school.

When I was twelve years old, Dad brought home his new date, Deleta, a pretty eighteen-year-old girl. Dell, as we all called her, was a girl I had often admired. A local girl, she had the most beautiful hair and a stunning figure. In a way I was happy for my father, but I dreaded the possibility that he would soon be moving out. I was right. Only three months later, Dad began building his new house more than two miles away.

After Dad moved out, Grandma took in three other grandchildren, including Dad's eighteen-year-old daughter, Esmie, and Uncle Reggie's two sons, Seymour, and Voris. My brother, Val, had just started school. I was happy for him, but it was depressing to watch all the other children going off to school. It was also a reminder that more than five years had passed since I had left school. Schooldays were a constant reminder that my hearing loss was keeping me confined to the home.

Around this time, Grandpa took sick. He had been ill before, but I never realized how serious his condition was until I overheard Grandma saying, "He doesn't have much longer to live." Not long afterward, Grandpa became bedridden. His hands and feet were swollen beyond their normal size and he couldn't walk. My job at the time was to help with whatever was needed when the family was away on the farm. When his condition took a turn for the worse, someone had to watch over him twenty-four hours a day.

I remember the day Grandma's brother, Uncle Teddy, arrived. There was talk that Grandpa was making his "last will and testament." I wondered what a last will and testament was.

Grandma, Uncle Reggie, and Uncle Teddy were all sitting in Grandpa's room, and I happened to arrive when my name was mentioned. Grandma insisted that the home would go to Uncle Everett, with her (Grandma), Aunt Vie, and Uncle Reggie having a life tenure to it. "What about Nita?" Grandpa asked. "I want her to have this room when I die."

"Nita is only a grandchild." Grandma said. "She has no right to any inheritance."

At that time it didn't bother me, but I didn't know what was coming next.

It was really sad to watch Grandpa's health deteriorate so rapidly. It was like watching him die slowly. At night, many of our neighbors volunteered to take turns sharing the weary night watch.

This was a period of great stress for me. Not only was my favorite grandfather dying, there was no peace or quiet in the home, especially at night, with so many people sitting around in the dark kitchen drinking coffee and smoking.

The night watch also attracted a lot of fun-seekers from all over the neighborhoods who had nothing better to do. While many of my friends and relatives gathered outside in the dark. I huddled inside the house where there was light from several gas lanterns. I felt helpless, knowing it would be impossible for me to communicate with anyone outside in the dark.

Then one night, the moon shone so brightly it was almost like day. I felt confident enough to go outside, knowing that some of my friends would be out there. I was looking for my friend Lucy when I spotted a group of older girls I had never seen before. A girl I knew named Lin came toward me. "These are my friends," she said. "They wanted to meet you." I nodded, not sure why they would want to meet me.

"Can you sing?" one of them asked. I shook my head, feeling pretty sure they were up to something. "Can you read?" the other girl asked.

"Yes," I nodded. Taking me by the hand Lin said, "I heard you can read the Bible very well. Let's go inside," she said, pointing toward the house. Once inside, one of the girls lured me into the corner of an empty room. With about six or seven girls gathered around me, I was pretty scared. Something in the way they were acting told me they were up to some mischief. Standing with my back to the wall, I was scared and tried to make some excuse, but before I could get away, one of the girls placed a Bible in my hands.

"You are not getting away until you read for us."

Helpless and unable to get away, I opened the Bible and began reading. Glancing at them every few seconds to see their reaction, I soon realized that my instincts were right. One of the girls was imitating me. "She talks funny," the other one said. The rest of them had their hands cupped over their mouth. I realized right away that they were making fun of me. Too embarrassed to do, or say anything, and feeling like the biggest fool in the world, I tried to walk away, but Lin held me back. "You have to finish this chapter."

It was a relief when my friend Lucy appeared and dragged me away. "I heard them," she said. "Those people are scum. Do you realize they were making fun of you?"

A few days later, Grandpa passed away. He was such a gentle human being that I was sure he went to heaven. The day before the funeral, I managed to sneak into the room where his body lay on the bed. As I gazed down at his lifeless body, looking so peaceful in sleep, I thought he must be in a place of rest. I placed my hands on his forehead and prayed. I don't remember the exact words I said, but I asked him to ask Jesus to help me to get my hearing back.

Unfortunately, not long after Grandpa died, I was sent to live with my father. I didn't want to go. I loved my father, but he never had any patience with me, and he rarely paid attention to me. Like so many family members, Dad was always annoyed whenever he had to repeat anything he said. "It's too much trouble talking to you," he angrily said one day. I felt so ashamed and helpless, but I had to admit that he was right. I found out, much to my annoyance, that relying on lipreading was not always accurate.

As I got older, I realized that most of the words we speak are invisible on the lips. And with so many look-alike words, I could only guess what others were saying. I would often read a book or poem and repeat what I was reading. By watching my lips in the mirror, I came to realize that many of the words I was saying looked the same. But I also learned that I could often guess the missing words in a complete sentence.

I also became skilled at pretending I was following what others were saying, when, in fact, I was only getting a word here and there. But it was better than having others repeating what they said and getting frustrated with me.

I kept hoping that Grandma would change her mind and let me stay with her. I knew that Grandpa wanted me to stay in his room. He had told me so before he died.

I managed to stall for several weeks, refusing to go until Grandma got angry. She stood before me, her hands on her hips. "I have enough grandchildren living in this house. Pack your things and go to your father."

I felt a sudden stab of pain as I gathered my few belongings into a plastic bag and walked out into the burning noonday sun. I didn't look back, and I didn't say goodbye. I was crying too hard. Of all the grandchildren living with Grandma, I couldn't understand why I was the only one she wanted to leave. For a long time, I was jealous of my cousin Audley because I knew he was Grandma's favorite. He had everything I didn't have. He had his mom and dad, Aunt Lora and Uncle Sydney, who loved him very much; and now that Grandma wanted me to leave, I was heartbroken.

Living with Dad was very different from the life I had at Grandma's. It was hard work. I spent every day running errands, gathering firewood, and carrying endless buckets of water. Since my father didn't have a water tank, I had to get our water from several of the neighbors. I was always exhausted by the end of the day, and I looked forward to the night when I could get some rest. I missed my friends and playmates at Grandma's, and I missed the kids whose little dresses I had been sewing for more than three years, and who gave me so much happiness.

I stayed with my father for two years, until I was called back to stay with Grandma. By then, I was sixteen years old and definitely felt grown-up. I felt wiser and more mature than when Grandma sent me away.

With most of her children and grandchildren gone, I was aware that Grandma really needed someone to help her with the housework, and I could tell she was very happy to have me back. The first thing she did was to take my hand and lead me straight to my Grandfather's room—which was still unoccupied. "Nita, this is your room. Your Grandpa always wanted you to have this room."

I nodded. I wanted to hug her, I was so overcome with gratitude at the thought of having my own room. But knowing that Grandma was not the kind to hug or show emotion, I simply said, "Thank you, Grandma."

Happy to be back at Grandma's, I wanted to do all the things I wasn't able to do when I was at Dad's. As soon as I settled down, I turned my attention to grooming myself. I was badly sunburned from working out in the burning tropical sun, and I wanted to get my complexion back to normal. I wanted to look like some of my friends who had been to Kingston and came back with flawless-looking skin and beautifully groomed hair. Angela was one of my first truly elegant city friends. After six months in Kingston, she came to visit me, well groomed and immaculately dressed. She looked like some of the models I had seen in fashion magazines.

I began bathing two times a day. By working out a simple skin care routine and following it faithfully, I was able to see results in a few weeks. My complexion became clear and free of sunburn and blemish, and I was happy with my appearance and my figure. I could tell my friends were beginning to notice because I was getting a lot of compliments. However, some of those compliments turned out to be very annoying. Too many times, they would comment, "She would be beautiful if only she could hear." Or they would say, "She is very pretty, but, poor thing, no man is going to marry her." And so it went, on and on, all ifs and buts.

Still, I was aware that looking my best was important, and I was determined to make the best of what I had. I had left my mother's sewing machine at Grandma's house when I went to stay with Dad. So, in addition to grooming myself, I made two dresses for myself. One Sunday, I decided to wear one of the dresses. I selected the royal blue dress—my favorite color. It was a simple, form-fitting dress with a detached peplum and a slit up to my left knee. To my surprise, this was the dress that attracted a lot of attention from my teenage friends and their parents who were visiting.

In the two years I had been away from Grandma's, a lot of changes had taken place. Audley, a brilliant student, had done very well in school and was getting ready to leave home for a college in Kingston within the next two years. He had become the pride and joy of the whole family, and I was happy for him. Because Audley often studied late into the night, I took the opportunity to study with him without interrupting him. I felt it was my one and only chance to learn something from him before he left for college.

To my surprise, Audley seemed genuinely happy to have my company, and I was grateful for the privilege to learn from his many books. He was one of the few people in the family who really encouraged me to get an education. He was willing to share his books and give me valuable advice. To this day, I remain grateful to him for his understanding and support.

Grandma had been suffering from failing eyesight around this time, but she refused to see a doctor, preferring to rely on faith and prayer for healing. Unfortunately, within a year she was completely blind in one eye. My responsibilities at the time were mainly taking care of housework and helping with the cooking and the laundry. But with Audley and Val going to school, and studying at night, it became my responsibility to read Grandma's mail and write back letters to her many relatives and grandchildren living abroad.

In the spring of 1953, with our annual country festival coming up, I was surprised that many of the local girls wanted me to make their dresses. For me, it was a welcome change from making children's clothes.

The annual festival was a time for the local girls to show off their dresses. The problem was that each girl wanted something unique to wear to the fair. I wanted badly to please all the girls, so I began doing a lot of sketching just to make sure that each girl had her own exclusive design. I must have made three dozen dresses in six weeks. It was a very exciting and busy time. I was thrilled to work with so many beautiful materials. For me, it was a wonderful opportunity to be sewing for most of the girls I had long thought were better off than me.

Because many of the girls were wearing dresses that I had designed for them, Grandma allowed me to go to the festival. I was excited but also dreaded the reaction of so many people. I worried about my speech and my voice. I wished I had the confidence to walk and talk like all the girls I had been sewing for. But I felt a sense of exhilaration when I saw how beautiful those girls looked in their dresses. I was giddy with happiness. I thought I was dreaming. I couldn't believe I was capable of making such beautiful dresses.

That day at the festival proved to be a real asset for me. In the following months, I was swamped with requests from almost every family for miles around. In a short time, I had become popular with many of the girls in and around the district. They were wonderful girls, generous and grateful for the dresses I made for them. And I became very close friends with all of them.

Before long, many of the local girls wanted to learn dressmaking. The biggest problem was getting Grandma's permission to teach in her home. I knew that some of the girls were planning to go to high school or college. But for the majority, that was out of the question. So the next best thing, as those girls jokingly put it, was, "learning to cook and sew—and then get married."

Grandma eventually agreed to allow me to teach in her home, but she laid down some very strict rules. I had to agree to a trial arrangement. I would have to take over the complete care of the house and the family laundry. I would teach only six girls at a time. I think Grandma was happy once I agreed, though, because the arrangement would leave her free to do her gardening job full time. As for me, this was a wonderful opportunity, and I sailed into my housekeeping trial with a fierce determination to succeed.

In the weeks that followed, I busily prepared for my teaching job. I changed the curtains. I waxed the floor until it shone a bright mahogany color. I covered the large dining table in the living room with a clear plastic cover to prevent scratching, so I could use it as a cutting table for pattern layout.

It was wonderful teaching those girls. It made my drab, lonely life came alive. We had so much fun laughing and talking. But like all girls, they loved to talk about love and romance. They were always bringing romantic books and magazines. I loved reading those books. It was like reading other people's life stories, and I wished I could write my own story.

What I didn't realize, though, was how annoying this was for Grandma. One day after the girls left, I was putting away the sewing supplies when she walked in. Hands on hips, she looked angry as she confronted me. "Can't you shut those girls up?"

"What do you mean?" I asked. I wasn't sure I knew what she was talking about.

"Do you know all the noise those gals are making?"

"You mean the girls talk too loud?"

Grandma shook her head. "It's really a good thing you can't hear all the noise they are making."

I had nothing more to say, so Grandma went on talking. "All they talk about is boys."

I shrugged my shoulders. "I wasn't talking about boys."

"You are not supposed to," she said. "If your father ever finds you talking about boys, he will beat you with a belt strap."

Looking back now, I shudder to think what my life would have been like if it weren't for my job and the wonderful girls who became my friends. I was aware that my job enabled me to fight a courageous battle against deafness and the prejudice it so often engenders. It wasn't long before I realized that I had more friends than my hearing friends themselves.

Being the only deaf girl in a community of thousands of people had made me feel that I had to be extraordinarily skillful to gain the respect of hearing people. As a young girl who had achieved professional prestige among my peers, I felt duty-bound to conduct my personal life with dignity. The fact that so many of the young girls were willing to let me teach them gave me a lot of confidence in myself.

Grandma wasn't the only one who was unhappy that I was teaching dressmaking to the local girls. Several of my customers wanted to make sure that their dresses were not going to be a part of the teaching process. I had a hard time assuring them that each girl brought her own material to make her own dresses. In the end, I decided that it was best to limit the teaching to two days per week.

Around this time, Dad announced that he was getting married. It wasn't surprising; I had expected this announcement all along. I knew

Dad was madly in love with Dell, and as far as I was concerned, they had been talking about marriage from the very beginning of their friendship. I eagerly looked forward to the wedding. I bought myself a pair of shoes and a matching hat, well in advance of the wedding, and I made myself a dress to go with everything.

But on the day before the wedding, I began to have second thoughts. I began to feel uneasy. I kept remembering stories I had heard about my mother, and the unhappy life she had had as a single parent, struggling to raise my sister and me. I had been told that my mother died of a broken heart after giving birth to my brother Val. I had always been told that my father didn't love my mother, that he refused to marry her, even when she was expecting their third child. I wanted to go to my mother's grave to weep, to let her know I was there for her.

So on the morning of the wedding, as I watched Grandma getting ready for Dad's wedding, I couldn't make up mind to go. I dilly-dallied around all morning, telling her that I would definitely join her for the wedding reception, but that I would not be attending the church service. My excuse was that the dress I had made was a very informal cotton dress and, that it would not be suitable for a church service.

When Grandma returned from the reception, she told me, "Your father will never forgive you." She then looked at me harshly. "You better go and see him and tell him you are sorry."

Of course I felt awful that I didn't go. But I knew I couldn't explain to her how, or why, I couldn't make up my mind to go. I didn't intentionally mean to hurt my father on his wedding day.

The following Sunday I went to see my father with the intention of telling him I was sorry I had missed his wedding. I felt a sense of relief that I didn't have to say anything. Dad didn't seem to care; he had nothing to say, and that was good for me.

Shortly before my eighteenth birthday, I realized that for me nothing would ever be the same. Everything had changed in the two years since I started doing dressmaking. Time seemed to travel like a speeding train that was taking me nowhere in life. It seemed that not a week went by that I wasn't saying goodbye to a friend or relative who was going off to high school or college. This was also the age when most of my friends began dating. I had long before accepted the fact that dating and marriage were for hearing people and not for me. The other girls teased me about not having a boyfriend, and a few of them had tried to set me up with dates. I didn't really didn't care about having a boyfriend; I was more concerned with having a career. Besides, I was still hoping for a miracle to get my hearing back. Many of my friends had fallen in love, and some of them had married very young, lost their youth and their figure to motherhood, and were struggling to raise their families.

I knew my father and grandmother were concerned about some of my friends who constantly talked about their boyfriends. Perhaps that's why they often lectured me, setting out a series of things they said I couldn't do:

"People like you have no right to talk about boys."

"You can't be like your friends. It's okay for them but not for you."

"You can't be like Angie and Margaret. They can hear, but you can't."

"No hearing man is going to marry you. They will only use you for your body and your money."

"Your sewing machine is the only husband you will ever have."

"If you had children, you couldn't take care of them. You couldn't teach them to talk."

In a way, I felt my family was just trying to protect me, but they didn't have to keep ramming everything down my throat. The truth is, I couldn't imagine falling in love with any of the young men in our district, or the surrounding districts of Treasure Beach and Southfield. In fact, most of the young men I knew were related to either my father or mother, often with the same surname. It was not unusual for many of the girls I grew up with to marry men with the same surname. I could never imagine falling in love with someone I had known all my life, someone I had grown up with.

"I promised myself never to get involved with any of these guys." I told one of my friends who was trying to set me up with a date.

"Anyway," she was saying, "you will have to find a man someday."

I looked at her, puzzled, wondering what on earth she was up to. But she only smiled. "Before you know it, you will be an old maid like your aunt Vie and your cousin Rosa." I just laughed; it didn't bother me one bit.

Aunt Vie and cousin Rosa were the talk of the district because they were single in their late thirties, had never been married, or even had a boyfriend.

I knew some of my friends were sorry for me because I didn't have a boyfriend. I knew many of them couldn't think of anything else they wanted to do except get married. It seemed that the most important thing in life for them was to fall in love, get married, and live happily ever after. But I had seen enough heartbreak among my friends to know that romance and marriage wasn't always a "bed of roses."

I didn't have to worry about getting dates. Many of the local boys had tried to get friendly with me, telling me how much they admired me, how they kept dreaming about me, and professing to fall helplessly in love with me.

"Don't ever believe any of them," Grandma kept warning me. "These men only want to trap you for your body and your money," she went on. "Did you ever hear of a hearing man marrying a deaf woman? You are very successful, but your sewing machine is the only husband you will ever have, and you should thank God he provided that for you."

Around this time, there was a guy who kept coming to our home. I know he liked me because he was always sending me notes. I think he was probably aware of how strict my grandmother was, and he needed a reason for coming by so often. So he pretended he was interested in buying one of the cows. One day, after he left, Grandma said to me, "Can you tell me why Jay (not his real name) is coming here every Sunday?"

"How would I know?" I said, frowning. "I don't even talk to him."

"Well," she said, "That's because he doesn't have a chance to talk to you. Do you think I would ever let you out of my sight when he is here?"

I sat there taking in everything, but decided not to make any comment. After awhile Grandma, said. "He's been coming here too often."

"Why don't you ask him what he wants?" I said finally.

She looked at me, winked, and said. "He is talking about buying a cow."

"Which cow is he interested in buying?" I asked.

"Nita, come to your senses. Jay has no interest in any cow but you."

I burst out laughing. Grandma was always so serious; it was refreshing to share a joke with her once in a while.

CHAPTER 5

The Educational Years

M Y LIFE HAD taken on a new meaning. After more than two years as a seamstress and nearly two years of teaching, I had gained a lot of confidence in my abilities. I had worked hard and earned the respect of those around me.

My newfound confidence helped me in ways I hadn't anticipated. One lesson I learned was that when I approached others with confidence, they were more likely to understand me than when I was timid and fearful. Communicating with others was possibly my most valuable asset.

Although my ability to lip-read made it possible for me to communicate normally with my family, friends, and customers. At the same time, I realized that I still had a lot to learn about lipreading and the differences in the way people speak. I found out that, while I could read most people's lips, even strangers, there were people whose lips I could not read at all. It was sad to realize that I couldn't understand a word my Uncle Easton was saying, and I didn't know why. I realized that lip-reading is somewhat like handwriting. Some people's handwriting is very hard to read, while others' are very easy to read.

I also realized that not everyone knew I was reading their lips. One day, I had a surprise visit from my friend Angie, whom I hadn't seen for some time. She was with a guy she had met in college. As usual, I was I was a bit intimidated when meeting someone new, but Ron was very friendly and easy to talk to. After a while, I felt relaxed and found that we had plenty to talk about. The next day when Angie came back to say goodbye, she asked, "Nita, how did you like my friend Ron?"

"He seemed very nice," I said, wondering what was coming next.

She smiled. "Ron thinks you are in love with him."

"Why would he think that?" I asked.

Angie just smiled and said, "Ron said no girl ever looked at him the way you did."

I could have died of embarrassment. But then I understood—maybe Ron didn't know that I had to read his lips; maybe he thought I could hear a little. How I wished I could go back to my hearing days, where I didn't have to read people's lips, where I could look the other way and listen to what others had to say.

Since I was working and earning money, I wanted to buy a new sewing machine. I was still using my mother's sewing machine, the old hand-spindle type, for all my dressmaking. I needed something that would make my job easier to manage. When Bernice, a friend of mine, offered to sell me a sewing machine that her mother had bought for her, I agreed to buy it. But I knew I would have to get permission from my father and grandmother first.

When I told Grandma about it, she gave me a strange look. "Nita," she said, "that kind of machine is very expensive. Where will you get the money to pay for it?"

I told her I had saved enough to pay for it, but she and my father were both opposed. When Bernice showed me the instruction book with all the features of the machine, I knew I had to have it. It was the latest model from the Singer Sewing Machine Company, and I knew it would make my work so much easier by freeing up both of my hands to guide the fabric. Even though Dad and Grandma did their best to discourage me, I went ahead and brought it. It turned out to be a great investment; and the machine had actually paid for itself after a year.

Between sewing for my many customers, teaching two days a week, and studying at night, I had no time for self-pity. I had no time to think about my hearing problems, and I was glad of that. I was doing something constructive, earning a little money, and at the same time improving my education. I had no formal training and no one to rely on, but I wanted to learn as much as possible. I saw education as a way to get ahead in life, a way out of my drab country life. Most of the better-off people I knew were well-educated, while most of the locals who worked as farmers were poor and unable to read or write. I figured that without education, I would end up like them.

Shortly after I turned nineteen, my cousin Audley left home to attend Wall-grove College in Kingston. After he left I became very restless. He was the only one who really encouraged me to improve my education, and I missed studying with him at night. Around this time, I was saying goodbye to many of my friends who were leaving home. Perhaps it was these feelings of loneliness and restlessness that led me to apply for a correspondence course, in the hope of getting a high school diploma. I was desperate to learn whatever I could, and I borrowed all the high school books I could get my hands on. I had the most difficulty with math. I just couldn't figure out the complex problems on my own, and I had no one to help me. After a time, I gave up on math and channeled my energy into learning other subjects.

Not surprisingly, Grandma was angry and discouraging when she found that out that I was taking a corresponding course. "What would you need a high school diploma for?" she asked. I wished she would encourage me instead of being angry with me. For some time, I had been writing all her letters to her relatives abroad. She always told me what to write, word for word. Her letters to her other grandchildren, nieces, and nephews, were full of encouragement about getting a good education and going to college before getting married. I had hoped that she would at least encourage me to study.

"Don't forget, all your friends are going to college because they can hear," she said. I stood there, saying nothing, so Grandma went on with her lecture. "Education is for hearing people who need to work. You don't need this kind of thing."

I wished I could explain to Grandma why education was so important to me, but she seemed to have her own vision of what my life should be like. She wanted me to be content with my life as it was, but I had other ideas—secret hopes and dreams. I refused to accept being consigned to a quiet, uneventful life, without any hope of going anywhere, or seeing the world.

I knew that Dad and Grandma had my life all planned, and they outlined it for me. According to Grandma, I could live in her home as long as she and Aunt Vie were alive. After they died, some family member would take me in and care for me. Dad and Grandma laid down strict rules for me, reminding me that people like me had no right to go anywhere, or do anything on our own. "You can't walk on the street," they told me. "You will always need someone to take care of you." I felt like a prisoner, walled off from the world.

As a very independent person, I resented their vision of my life. I was determined not to let them hold me back from doing the things I wanted to do. I vowed to make the best of what I had, and to live my life as normally as possible. As a young adult, I had come to realized that the biggest barrier in my life was not deafness, but my family's views of it. To my family, hearing loss was a major handicap, and they wanted me to see it that way. I told them that "handicapped" people are people who need physical assistance. "People with hearing loss never need physical assistance." I said. I kept looking at myself in the mirror just to assure myself that I was normal. I felt normal, I knew I looked normal, and I had never needed physical assistance. That was enough to give me some consolation. But shortly after my nineteenth birthday, Dad and Grandma began delivering a series of long lectures on all the things they believed I was incapable of doing. I felt as if I had been stabbed in the heart when they told me that I didn't need a name. I never understood why my family made such an issue of my name. It was like saying that I didn't need an identity as a person. All I wanted was for them to accept me as a person with the same rights as anyone else. But they insisted that because I couldn't hear I didn't need an identity. The hardest thing to accept was when they told me that I would never be able to travel, or do anything requiring a name. I loved my family and I looked to them for advice and support. It would have meant the world to me just to know that that I was a person to them, but the things they said gave me nothing but heartbreak.

Telling this part of my life story in detail would hurt too many people dear to me. Only God knows the pain and suffering I endured. I went through a period of deep depression from which I never fully recovered. My family had left me without any hope of going out in the world and making a name for myself. Although they tried to reassure me that, without a name, I had nothing to lose, I made it clear to them that no matter what happened, my name was my birthright and no one was going to take it away from me.

I firmly believed that God would be there for me, that He would carry me through my stress and pain. By the grace of God, I prayed for the only thing that really mattered to me at that time—getting my hearing back as easily as it went away.

I had long since given up hope that my family would take me to get my hearing tested, and I knew that I had to help myself. Both Grandma and Dad remained strictly opposed to any medical evaluation or treatment. But I had seen many advertisements for hearing aids, and I hoped to find a doctor who could prescribe one. I knew, though, that as long as I lived with Grandma, I would never have the opportunity to have my hearing tested.

Around this time, I began to see Aunt Vie as a friend. As a child, I had viewed her as just another adult in the home who gave orders. But when we got our first radio, Aunt Vie was very excited. She became the most ardent radio listener in the home, getting up at four o'clock in the morning to listen to a *Back to the Bible* broadcast, and other religious programs. One Sunday morning, I was taken by surprise when she came into my room with a Bible in her hands. I was sitting up in bed reading a magazine. As I looked into her face, a face that was always so sad, for the first time I noticed how happy she looked.

"Nita," she began, "I can't tell you how happy I am. I have found peace with God. I am born again." She went on to tell me that she had been listening to a *Back to the Bible* broadcast, and that the message had changed her life. She walked toward me and handed me the Bible. "Please read Galatians 2:20." After I read the verse for her, she said, "Nita, I wish you could hear the sermon on the radio; the music and the singing are so wonderful!" After a pause, she added, "Don't worry, I will tell you everything I hear on the radio, and you can read the Bible for me."

I was filled with happiness for her. "Let's make a deal," I said brightly. She hugged me then, and from that day we became good friends, sharing a need that would help us both.

Although I was successful in many things, my social life was a mess. I can well remember the day I went to a country fair with some friends. We were all sitting on a park bench laughing and talking when, suddenly, the music started and everyone got up to dance. I watched my friends as they danced to the beat of the drums. I was deep in thought and didn't see the young guy who had come and sat next to me. He must have said something before I was aware of his presence.

"Would you like to dance?" I caught him saying.

"I am sorry," I said, wishing he would go away. "I have a headache."

He smiled, "It's pretty hot. Maybe a cool drink can help."

"Thanks," I said. "But I don't need anything."

He sat there, talking to me and carrying on a lively conversation. I, of course, had to watch his lips. I had become so accustomed to watching people's lips that I didn't think anything of it. When my friends came back, they were laughing and giggling.

"What's so funny?" I asked, but they continued laughing and winking.

"So you got a boyfriend?" Etta, one of my friends, finally said,

"Who?" I asked.

"We saw you talking to that nice guy. He thinks you are in love with him."

By then, I was pretty annoyed. "Why would he think that?"

"Well," Etta said, "we overheard him telling his friends that you are in love with him, that you never took your eyes off his face."

I knew immediately what had really happened, and I was embarrassed. The guy had not realized that I had a hearing problem and was reading his lips. Unfortunately, this became a major problem for me: boys seemed to think that I was in love with them because I was watching their lips. What was so funny for my friends was nothing but embarrassment for me.

Dealing with new customers was another hurdle I had to overcome. I usually explained to them that I had a hearing problem because I wanted them to feel comfortable when communicating with me. My speech was not a problem, and I knew strangers could understand me. I had been blessed with perfect hearing for the first seven years of my life, but after I lost my hearing I was very much aware of the stigma attached to deafness.

One day, I was fitting a dress on a new customer who lived in the city. As I bent to pin the hem of her dress, I realized that she must have said something to me when I wasn't looking. "Did you say something to me?" I asked. She nodded. "I am sorry, I didn't hear you. I have a hearing problem." She asked if I had ever tried a hearing aid. I told her I had not.

"Why not?" she asked. "I think a hearing aid would help you." She paused, then said, "As a matter of fact I know someone who wear two hearing aids and she seems to hear very well with them."

I felt the blood rush to my face. Breathlessly, I asked, "Do you know the name of the doctor who helped her?"

"No," she answered. "But if you like, I could get the doctor's address for you."

Two weeks later, she gave me a card with the address of Dr. Ainsley Dujon. I didn't know if he was a medical doctor or just a hearing aid dispenser. But I figured it was my one and only chance. I was desperate to find someone who could, at least, give me some helpful advice.

A couple of weeks later, I mailed a letter to Dr. Dujon requesting an appointment.

Two weeks later I got a reply. The appointment date was three months away, so I had plenty of time to think and make plans. Kingston was a long way to travel and I couldn't go there without a chaperone. I had four big hurdles to overcome. The first was getting my parents' consent; then finding someone willing to accompany me; and getting a place for the two of us to stay. Finally, I had to face the fact that the doctor fees, the bus fare back and forth for two, plus a place to stay for a couple of days was likely to eat up all my savings.

I read the letter to Grandma, hoping to win her help in persuading my father to let me travel to Kingston for the hearing aid evaluation.

When my father found out about it he was furious. "How do you expect a hearing aid to help you if you can't hear anything?" he demanded.

Finally, I turned to my mother's sister, my Aunt Lulu, the only person I thought would help me. Aunt Lulu and my cousin Audley arranged for us to stay with one of my cousins who lived in Kingston.

We arrived in Kingston late at night. To me, a country girl who had never been to the city before, Kingston was a beautiful city with dazzling lights. I felt happy as we walked along the street. I loved the many display windows adorned with beautifully dressed mannequins. I wanted to live and work in that beautiful city and be a part of it. I had spent so much of my life dreamed about living in the city.

The next day, I arrived for my appointment with Dr. Dujon, my heart filled with hope. Instead of the battery of tests I had expected, the doctor simply placed a light on my forehead, jingled a bunch of keys behind my ears, and that was the end of the test. It was over in less than two minutes. I watched in disbelief and dismay as the doctor sat in front of me, shaking his head as he talked with Aunt Lulu. I didn't need to be told anything. I knew he had bad news. As I got up to leave I found myself swaying and for an instant I thought I was going to faint. For me, the painful realization that I would never hear again was the end of the world, the end of all my hopes and dreams.

Later that day, I turned my thoughts to home. Facing my hostile father with the news that the doctor was unable to do anything to help me was more than I could bear. I had traveled to Kingston at my own expense so I hoped my father would at least be sympathetic since he had nothing to lose.

It was Saturday night when we reached home. I'd never been more tired in my life, but I couldn't sleep. I tossed and turned in my bed, wishing God would take me away. Worst of all, I knew I would have to face my father the next morning. He always visited Grandma on Sunday mornings.

I was standing by the window when I saw Dad coming down the footpath. Grandma went out to meet him. As they stood there talking, I could tell from where I was standing that they were talking about me. I managed to make out a few words.

"Where is she?" Dad was saying. "Where is the d——fool?"

I could feel a shudder of despair running through my body. *Oh God,* I thought, *how am I going to face my father?* I wished the floor could collapse and swallow me up. Silently I prayed, *Dear God, give me the courage to face my father.* I was still standing by the window when Dad walked in.

"You d——fool," he shouted at me. "Didn't I tell you not to go, spending every penny you worked so hard to get." He went on raving and cursing but I was in too much shock to observe what he was saying.

Somehow, I made it through the day. That night, lying in bed, I kept thinking about all the awful things my father had said to me. I felt that he could at least try to understand that I had no way of knowing if there was medical help for me unless I tried. Instead of getting angry, I thought he could at least sympathize with me. Suddenly, I was angry at my father for being so unreasonable. All he seemed to care about was the money I had lost. But money was not the most important thing in my life. And then, it dawned on me that losing all my money didn't matter to me. I felt that it was better to have tried and failed than to never have tried. With this knowledge, I consoled myself that I could look back on this day years later without any regrets. I was happy that I had not left undone something that later I would wish I had done,

It was almost morning when I finally fell asleep. The sun was shining through my bedroom window when I awoke. I got down on my knees and prayed, *dear God, whatever plans you have for me, help me to make it in this world.*

Later I walked outside. It was a bright and beautiful day. The air was cool and comforting, and surprisingly I was not sad at all. As I walked through the tall grass toward the hills, with the cool breeze streaming over me, I knew I was willing to accept God's plan for my life, even though I knew there would be a hard struggle ahead. I wandered aimlessly, enjoying the fresh air and the beautiful flowers that grew wild everywhere. Suddenly I had an impulse to climb the hills, something I had not done since I had lost my hearing more than twelve years before. I sat on a small rock, looking up at the hills. As I sat there, my thoughts drifted back to the days when my cousins and I played hide-and-seek in the hills and caves and the surrounding hideaways. I closed my eyes, and suddenly I was a seven-year-old again playing in the hills and caves. I could almost hear my playmates calling to me. I thanked God for such vivid and beautiful memories, which I knew would always be a part of my life.

Climbing the hills was not easy for me that day, but I pressed on until I reached the top. When I looked down at the path I had just crossed, I marveled at how I had managed to reach the top. There were many dangerous rocks and the narrow footpath was overgrown with thorns and thistles.

I stood there a long time knowing I would soon have to turn my attention to climbing back down. As I stood there looking back at the path I had just crossed, I began to see it as a symbol of my life. Standing on the top of the hill that day was a lesson for me, like looking back and seeing the path of my life, a life that was filled with obstacles and challenges. As I made my decision to climb down on the other side of the hills, I realized that the path before me was a challenge I still had to overcome. As I reached the bottom of the hills, I told myself that with God's help I would overcome all obstacles, no matter how many twists and turns the road in my life would take.

After this incident I wanted to devote my whole life to God, but I couldn't help feeling rebellious toward at my parents and I felt that my very faith in God was being challenged. I decided I had to do something to show my parents that I was not as helpless as they thought.

After weeks of planning, I decided to take a bus to Black River, the nearest city, to visit a friend who worked there. I didn't tell anyone. It was around four o'clock in the morning and still dark as I slipped quietly out the door, geared up for the long walk to the bus stop more than two miles away.

The walk seemed to go on forever, but it was refreshing to see the dawn breaking over the horizon. It felt good to be on my own, without anyone watching over me. Once I was on the bus, I looked around, hoping that no one would recognize me. I walked to the back of the bus and took a seat. When the bus reached the city, I panicked. I didn't even know where to get off until I saw most of the passengers leaving. I felt like the biggest fool in the world, as I stood on the sidewalk watching the cars whizzing by. Finally, I crossed the street to the department store where my friend Mazy worked. A man sitting at the desk asked, "Can I help you?"

"I am looking for Mazy," I said. "I think she works here." He told me Mazy was out to lunch so I decided to do a little shopping at the store next door. I was surprised by how easy it was for me to talk to people. It was my first real experience of being out on my own, and it gave me a lot of confidence.

My new-found confidence didn't last long. Grandma immediately contacted my father who promptly came to see me. During the confrontation he suddenly got up and slapped me across the face so violently that I fell halfway across the floor.

CHAPTER 6

End of a Dream

THE REMAINDER OF my teen years passed almost unnoticed as I worried about my future. So much had changed in the years since I had started doing dressmaking. Ready-to-wear dresses were becoming very popular, a fad among the local girls. I felt it was just a matter of time before I was out of a job. I still had enough customers to keep me working overtime, but I was worried about my future. Most of my friends had left home to attend college, and many of them had taken up residence in Kingston, in England, and in the United States.

As far as my prospects were concerned, I saw myself as a twenty-year-old woman without a name or the freedom to go anywhere on my own or make any decisions of my own. I felt that my family was treating me as a child by confining me at home. It was embarrassing to be chaperoned everywhere I went by family members who were often much younger than I was. I was frustrated with these restrictions but I knew there was nothing I could do about it. I felt doomed to a life of subjection. The only thing I could do was to plunge into my work as if my life depended on it.

On the brighter side, my students and customers provided constant company during the day. This connection with others was one of the most important things in my life. My friends abroad seemed to understand how lonely I was and they wrote me encouraging letters. Knowing how unhappy and lonely I was, many of my friends suggested that I reach out to others. "Why don't you join a pen-pal club since you can't go anywhere?" one of my friends suggested. "It will put some happiness into your life."

I was aware that many of the local girls had pen friends, but I wasn't sure I wanted to correspond with people I had never met.

"Nita, you listen to me," Caseta said to me one day. "I joined a worldwide pen pal club and I am getting some of the most wonderful letters from people all over the world." A few days later she handed me a large envelope full of letters. "Read these," she said.

I read quite a few of them. Some of them sounded pretty interesting, but some sounded crazy. "Do you answer all these letters?" I asked, alarmed.

"Only the most interesting ones," she said.

I shouldn't have been surprised a few months later when I started getting letters from people in the United States, England, Canada, and Europe. But after a time I lost interest. I figured I was wasting valuable time that could be put to more interesting things.

At this stage in my life, Aunt Vie was the only one in the home with whom I could really communicate without feeling inadequate. When I wasn't with my students or customers, she would often drop by my room for a chat, often with a Bible in her hands. Unfortunately she couldn't read or write, so I would read the Bible for her. She had a good knowledge of the Scriptures and would often tell me what chapter and verse in the Bible she wanted me to read for her. Aunt Vie was a firm believer in God, who like myself, was not allowed to go anywhere outside the home.

She was always talking about life after death, and how wonderful the next life would be. I could identify with her in many ways, and there were many times when I wanted to die peacefully. Unlike me, Aunt Vie was content to live in seclusion, she didn't mind being confined to the home.

But I saw things differently: I could not see myself, forever living a quiet uneventful country life.

At age twenty-five I took the opportunity to fulfill my lifelong desire to became a certified dress designer. Most of my original students had left home and their places were taken by their younger sisters. I applied for a home-study course in fashion design from the National School of Dress Design, a Chicago-based firm in the United States. I saw the advertisement in a magazine. The magazine presented an attractive layout describing a full course in costume designing, fashion sketching, pattern drafting, and cutting and fitting. I was hooked instantly.

Even though it was a home-study course, I found it very interesting. It provided an excellent practical education in the many ways to do costume designing. Best of all, I was able to improve my sketching and pattern drafting. I also learned various ways to do cutting and fitting. It was really exiting to know that what I was learning was actually the way people worked in the fashion industry around the world. I knew that I had to keep up with a rapidly changing world of fashions and trends, and I wanted to learn all the basic rules of dress designing and dressmaking.

The biggest challenge was keeping the home-study course a secret from Grandma. I did not want her to know that I was taking a dress design course because I knew she would not approve. I also knew she would have a fit if she found out I was doing something behind her back. We didn't have a rural mail carrier, so I had to rely on two of my students to mail and collect my parcels from the post office, at least every two weeks.

I had just started the dress design course when Aunt Vie took sick and had to be rushed to the hospital. Grandma became depressed and she took to her bed and could not be comforted. I spent all my spare time with her, but there was very little I could do beyond comforting her, praying with her, and getting her something to eat. After three days in the hospital, Aunt Vie died. She was forty-three years old.

I will never forget the day they brought her body home. It was a Sunday, and no public transportation was available. Grandma hired a car and my father and his wife volunteered to go. As usual, I stayed home with Grandma.

Normally a visit back and forth to the hospital by car should have taken less than two hours. By nightfall, Dad and Dell still hadn't returned and Grandma grew very alarmed.

There was nothing I could do so I went outside to wait. After a few minutes, I saw the headlights of a car turning in the direction of our home. As it neared the house, the headlights suddenly went off. As I stood there puzzled, I saw two shadowy figures running toward the house. They were Dad and Dell. They rushed past me into the house, took Grandma in their arms and hugged her. I didn't know what was going on. I watched as Grandma got up looking happy and relieved. She threw her hands up in the air and said, "Thank you Lord."

She walked over to the window, threw it open, and said, "Bring her in."

My first thought was that Aunt Vie had gotten better and was coming home. I went back outside to wait for the car. It came slowly up the driveway. The headlights were still turned off. Suddenly, the car stopped and the headlights came on. I went to the car, hoping to be the first to welcome Aunt Vie back home. Aunt Vie was not in the car. As I drew back, I saw a body bag tied to the top of the car, one foot sticking out. It was then I realized with a shock that Aunt Vie was dead. The sudden shock of seeing Aunt Vie's body was just too much for me. It took me months to get over her death.

For months I couldn't understand Grandma's reaction, or why she was so happy the day Aunt Vie died. The house had become a lonely place for me with only Grandma, Uncle Reggie, and myself. Except for my students and customers, there wasn't anyone with whom I could really hold a conversation.

I didn't realize how wrong I was about Grandma until late one night as I was getting ready for bed, I noticed that she was not in her bed. I went looking for her and found her sitting on the steps to her room. Her body was hunched over, so I went to check on her. She looked up, surprised, and I noticed that she was crying. "Are you feeling sick, Grandma?" I asked.

She didn't answer right away, but then she said, "You know I didn't cry when Vie died, I loved her so much." I nodded, and she went on. "I asked God to take her home and He did." She turned to face me. "Nita," she said. "If I had died before Vie, no one would want to take care of her." I hugged her and for the first time I felt I truly understand her. Maybe she was even praying for me. Maybe she wanted God to take me home also. I didn't want anyone to take care of me, but I didn't feel that I would ever need anyone. But then, Grandma might have thought otherwise.

It was a lonely life for me. I went to church occasionally on Sundays with Grandma, and after church she allowed me to visit my father. Dad had changed completely, and was a devoted husband and father to his young wife and four children. Unfortunately his visits to Grandma's home had dwindled almost to nothing. The only times I really saw him were when I visited him at his home. It would have meant the world to me if my father had something to say to me, but I never seemed to get his attention, and I always went home brokenhearted to the Grandma's lonely house.

About two years after Aunt Vie died, Grandma suffered a stroke. One side of her face was twisted, and she had problems getting in and out of bed. I was afraid that she might die, and prayed earnestly for her complete recovery. Once again I cancelled most of my working arrangements to care for her. I remember my father telling me, "It's your God-given duty to take care of your grandmother until she dies. After that someone will take you in and care for you."

Inwardly I felt rebellious. No one had any right to make that decision for me, I told myself. I knew the family didn't think that I should be on my own. Uncle Everett had inherited the family home when Grandpa died. He wanted to sell it but Grandma and Uncle Reggie had a lifetime tenure to the home. I figured I was only allowed to stay there as long as Grandma was alive. Grandma made an amazing recovery in six months and after that we became the best of friends.

At age twenty-eight, though, I was getting desperate. After being housebound for more than twenty years and after more than a decade of teaching a succession of sixteen- and eighteen-year-old girls, I was feeling pretty old. My students were never younger than sixteen or older than eighteen. I knew that most of my students would probably leave their parents' homes by the time they were nineteen, but I would still be in the same place, doing the same thing. I was aware that dressmaking was just a revolving door for most of the girls I was teaching. This was the pattern of life I had come to expect.

Like most of my friends, my cousin Audley had graduated from college long ago. A very successful bank manager and businessman, he quickly moved up the corporate ladder. I was really happy for him. He and his pretty young wife Eula, and their cute little son, Hugh, would often visit us at Grandma's. My brother Val was living and working in Kingston. I know it wasn't easy for him, and I wished with all my heart that I could help him. Like so many other students, Val managed to pay his tuition fees by working during the day and going to a commercial college at night.

As for me, I had my own problems to deal with. It was hard to live with the awful realization that I would probably never leave home. Instead of the bright future I had always dreamed about, stretching before me was a life of boredom and frustration. There was nothing I could do about it but pray for divine guidance and deliverance. I didn't believe that God wanted me to spend the rest of my life living in gloom. There were days when I was so depressed I wanted to withdraw from the whole world. The constant lectures from Dad and Grandma, a series of "you cant's," added to my depression. I became frustrated, confused, and rebellious, and for a long time I just couldn't pray. No matter how hard I tried to pray, I couldn't get rid of the rebellion in my heart but I kept hoping God would forgive me.

And then one morning I got the answer to my prayers. I remember lying in bed, wide awake and deep in thought, when suddenly I saw the vision of an angel standing at the foot of my bed. She nodded and vanished in a flash.

I lay still for a long time, not moving or breathing, wishing the angel would return. And then I began to wonder if it was a dream or a vision. Everything had happened so suddenly, I didn't have time to think. One thing I knew for sure, whether it was vision or dream, God surely wanted me to know that He had forgiven me. Suddenly I was on my knees, thanking God for answering my prayer. Never again would I ever doubt God. I got up feeling as light as a feather and ran into the kitchen to tell Grandma I had seen an angel.

"That was just a dream," Grandma said, shaking her head. "You dreamt you saw an angel."

To this day I still find it hard to believe that it was just a dream. It was so vivid, so unlike any dream I have ever had. But this incident will always live in my mind forever.

A week later, I told Grandma that I wanted to attend church with her. She was now a member of the Assembly of God Church, and she seemed genuinely happy to have me attending the services with her. After attending service for six weeks I agreed to be baptized. I was really happy in our church. We had three wonderful pastors: Brother Arnold, Brother Willie, and Brother Stephen.

A couple of months after I was baptized, I began having a strange pain in my right side. The pain got more intense every day. I knew I needed to see a doctor and I wished I had the freedom to see a doctor, but I couldn't go anywhere on my own. I kept telling Grandma about the pain I was having in my side, but all she said was, "Don't worry. It's just wind. It will pass." As the weeks went by, however, the pain became unbearable. One night I couldn't sleep, the pain was so intense that I curled up in a fetal position. I knew then that something was seriously wrong with me and that I needed to see a doctor. I was twenty-eight years old and I had not been to a medical doctor since I had left the hospital more than nineteen years earlier.

I will never forget the day my father took me to the doctor. If I live to be a hundred, I will not be able to understand his frustration with me. Apart from the pain in my side everything seemed normal as we walked the two miles to the bus stop. He didn't say a word. But as we stood waiting for the bus, he looked angrily at me. "When you get on the bus don't look at anyone or say anything to anyone, if anyone says something to you just do this," he said as he touched his ears and lips. "Don't talk to anyone. Your voice is strange and no one is going to understand you."

When we reached the city, we walked to the doctor's office a few blocks away. As we entered the doctor's office, Dad pointed to a chair for me to sit. He went and sat on the opposite side of the room. Pretty soon, a woman came and sat in the empty seat beside me. She said something but I didn't get what she said. Since I was not supposed to speak, I touched my ears and lips. I looked helplessly at my father, hoping he would say something. But he just acted indifferent. The woman looked at me and said, "You are a selfish thing."

When it was my turn to see the doctor, Dad got up and beckoned for me to follow. As he turned around, I caught him saying, "Doctor, I am not your patient. The one behind me is your patient." Dad sat with his back to me as he talked to the doctor so I couldn't tell what he was saying. Neither of them looked in my direction, and I felt humiliated when Dad motioned for me to go into a room and undress. The doctor made a brief examination and released me. I couldn't wait to get out of there. But that was not the end of my disappointment. As we walked back to the bus stop, I asked Dad, "What did the doctor say?"

"Nothing's wrong with you," he said harshly. "You better stop complaining about pain because I have no time to waste taking you to any doctor."

I must have died a thousand deaths. I couldn't believe what he was saying. I couldn't believe he was talking to me like that. What did I do? I was often in pain and he was telling me the doctor said nothing was wrong with me. What did he tell the doctor anyway?

As we walked back to the city, I saw our bus parked on the side of the road. "Well," Dad said pointing to the bus, "You have to stay in that bus."

I glanced at my watch, it was only eleven thirty, the pain wasn't so bad, and I wanted to shop around in the stores. I know that the bus was a passenger bus that took people to work in the city, and it would not be leaving until the day shift was over. "The bus is not leaving until four thirty." I said to Dad.

"Listen," Dad said angrily, "You can't walk on the street. You can't hear."

I realized it was useless to argue with Dad so I finally gave in. Waiting in the bus was like an eternity. It was stifling hot with every window and door closed. I managed at length to open a window. But I just couldn't relax with Dad's angry words going through my mind. I suddenly began to see things differently for the first time in my life. I began to feel that my father was ashamed of me, that I was some sort of embarrassment to him. I was angry with him for the way he carried on.

Meanwhile, back at home the pain in my side was getting more intense and more frequent. But the agony in my heart was just as painful. I knew

I would rather die than go through the humiliating experience with my father a second time. Three weeks later, I was preparing some fashion sketches. It was late at night and everyone had gone to bed. Suddenly I felt a paralyzing pain in my side. I immediately dropped my sketches and headed for my room, but I could not get to my bed. I collapsed on the floor. Later I managed to pull myself up onto the bed by gripping the mattress. I lay in bed, unable to sleep, and toward daylight I began throwing up. I couldn't tell what had happened to me, but after lying there for a few minutes I realized that I couldn't lift my feet.

It must have been close to midday when Grandma returned from her gardening job and noticed I wasn't up to make the beds. Lucky she was with a neighbor who took one look at me and said to Grandma. "You will have to get her to a hospital right away. She is blue." So I was back in the doctor's office after less than a month. The moment he touched my tummy I jumped, the pain was so intense.

"She has a ruptured appendix and will need surgery," the doctor said to Grandma. "I am sending her to the hospital right away."

As they put me to sleep, I hoped that I would never wake up from the surgery. The past three weeks of pain had drained me of all energy and hope, and all I wanted was to rest forever from the pain.

I awoke from the surgery with the most intense pain I had ever felt in my life. I couldn't move; every breath I took was painful. But in the midst of the pain, I looked up to see my father standing by my bedside. I felt a flood of tears pouring down my face as he said, "You will be all right," but I couldn't say a word. I could barely breathe, much less talk.

Back at home, I had to cancel all my sewing and teaching work. I had gained a lot of weight and felt completely out of shape, but I really didn't care. I had temporarily lost my taste for the things of the world. The experience at the hospital where I was chloroformed for the surgery had changed me completely. My tummy looked like it had been cut in two and stitched together again. I wanted to devote all my time to helping myself recover both in mind and body. It no longer bothered me that my family had no confidence in me. After years of trying I had given up expecting to win their confidence. It seemed that no matter how decently I had conducted my personal life they just wouldn't see the real me, all they seemed to see was the deafness.

There were days when I could no longer daydream of far-away places. Kingston was a place I had visited only once. I had always wanted to live there because the night was almost as bright as day, a stark contrast to the dark country farm where we lived. To me Kingston was a place where I would never be afraid to walk outside at night with a friend. The countryside was always dark and I would never dare to walk outside at night with friends. But at this stage in my life I had to face the stark reality that all my hopes and wishes might turn out to be just a dream that could never come true.

Life for me might have gone on this way forever if it wasn't for Nulis Barnett, one of my best customers and a good friend of mine who was away at a college in Mandeville. A few weeks after I received my certificate from the National School of Dress Design, I got a letter from Nulis. She wrote to thank me for the dresses I had made for her. "My landlady," she wrote, "is very impressed by the dresses you made for me. She thinks you have a special talent in dressmaking and would like to meet you."

Nulis went on to say that her landlady, Mrs. Darcy Hudson (who was also her cousin), thought I would be more successful in the city than the country. Nulis persuaded me to take a trip to Mandeville. I didn't know how to approach my father to ask his permission let me visit Mandeville. Knowing my father, I dreaded the possibility of an outburst. The best I could do was to plead with Grandma to talk to my father.

Almost a month later, I got a surprise visit from Dad and his wife, Dell. I had been outside cutting some ballad plants to make a broom. (The ballad broad, velvety leaves was my favorite broom for sweeping the floor. It leave the mahogany floor shiny and dust–free.) "Nita," Grandma said as I came through the door, "This meeting is going to be a big surprise for you."

I didn't know what to expect, but I had the uneasy feeling that the meeting had been arranged by Grandma for the purpose of questioning me about a recent trip I had made to Black River without her permission.

"Well." Dad began, "Dell will be going to Mandeville next Saturday. You can go with her, and she will try to find out all she can about the lady you want to meet."

I wanted to get up and hug each of them, but guilt had replaced the resentment I felt, so I just sat there looking at each of them for confirmation. They were all smiling.

The prospect of living and working in Mandeville gave me a feeling of excitement and dread at the same time. But this was an opportunity I couldn't afford to miss. I saw it as my one and only chance. I was a nervous wreck all week, as I planned what to wear, what to say, and how to present myself. I had no confidence in my speech. My biggest fear was that Mrs. Hudson, the lady who was going to interview me, would not be able to understand me, and I was afraid I would stumble over my words. My family had instilled in me the belief that strangers could not understand me, so I was always nervous about speaking to strangers.

I was still in this uncertain state of mind when Dell and I arrived at the Hudson Appliance store on Park Place. But the moment I met Mrs. Hudson, I felt a deep sense of calm. She greeted me warmly and I didn't have any problems understanding her. Even better, she understood me perfectly. The meeting went well with her and her husband Thomas, who sat in on the interview. Afterward, she showed us the rooms upstairs. There were two rooms available, and I chose the larger one with two big windows and a view of the street below. Mrs. Hudson told me that I could move in within two weeks if I wanted the room.

Back at home, I told Grandma that I was planning to move. "Nita," she said, "Come to your senses. How can you expect to do business in Mandeville? You can't hear; who is going to understand you?" I didn't want to argue with her and I knew I still had one big hurdle to overcome—getting my father's approval.

I was in luck. Dell was on my side and that made it easier for me to win my father's approval. Dad and Dell even offered to let Juliet, their fourteen-year-old daughter, stay with me for a couple of weeks.

So far, everything was set, and I began planning the move. I didn't know where to begin, or who would transport my sewing machine and other heavy sewing equipment. But once word got around that I was leaving, our church pastors all pitched in to give me help and valuable advice. Brother Arnold offered to loan me his van. He and Brother Stephen informed Brother Hall who pastured our church in Mandeville that I would be joining his church in Mandeville. I was very grateful and pleased with all the arrangements.

Finally, moving day came. The night before, I couldn't sleep. Slowly, I looked around the room, knowing I was going to miss this place. Everything about my room reminded me how safe and sheltered I felt at Grandma's. Now I was going out into the great unknown. I sat down on my bed and prayed, my heart filled with sadness and guilt. How long I sat there I don't really know.

I got up and looked out the window. The moving van had arrived, and the men were loading my belongings into the van. Grandma was standing by the van; she looked old and haggard, as if she had aged overnight. I felt tears begin to pour down my face. *Oh God,* I thought, *I just can't say goodbye to her.* Angrily, I wiped the tears from my eyes. I had to move on, I had to find the courage to let go. I picked up my bags and hurried out.

The agony I felt must have showed on my face because Grandma walked toward me with her arms outstretched.

"Don't worry, darling," she said, looking into my tearful eyes. "You can come back anytime, but I hope you will get this silly idea about leaving out of your head."

CHAPTER 7

Letting Go

THE DAY I moved to Mandeville was a bright, sunny January morning in 1966. It should have been a happy day for me—I had looked forward to this day for so long. I would finally be free to be my own person, free to make my own decisions. But I had a heavy heart filled with sadness and guilt. I was torn between my need to be free and my loyalty to my grandmother. Even though Uncle Reggie was still living with Grandma, I couldn't get over feeling guilty about leaving her at a time when she needed me most. Of all the painful decisions I had to make, leaving Grandma was one of the most difficult.

I arrived at the Hudson Appliance store late in the afternoon, and was greeted warmly by Mrs. Hudson and her two daughters, Patsy and Marge. The welcome helped put my mind at east and take away some of the doubts I was experiencing about my decision to leave home. Mr. Hudson had sent his chauffer, Ken, to pick me up after my things had been unloaded from the van and put away. It didn't take long for me to realize that they were a true Christian family. They lived a godly life and practiced what they preached. I felt truly blessed to have met them. I immediately noticed their generosity and hospitality. In less than a week, I felt as if I had known them all my life. I wasn't surprised to learn that Mr.

Hudson was the pastor of a local church. I went to church with the family the first Sunday I was there. I would gladly have joined their church, but I had already met with Brother Easton Hall, the pastor of my church in Mandeville, and he had arranged to pick me up every Sunday morning.

The Hudsons owned and operated an appliance store on Park Place. It was in one of the busiest parts of the city, and I felt very lucky that they had rented me the office overlooking the street, above their shop. It was the perfect place to start a business. In addition to the room at their shop, I also had a room at the family residence on Villa Road, which was about five minutes outside the city.

I spent my first five days in Mandeville distributing my business cards and getting to know the city. I was only too aware that I was a country-bred farm girl who had been protected from the outside world all my life. I had to quickly adjust to the fast-paced city life. Walking along the street, I was thrilled to see the many display windows adorned with beautifully dressed mannequins, and well-dressed women on the street.

I also realized that there were many well-established dressmakers in Mandeville and that I would have to do my best work in order to compete with them. I worried that I would not succeed as a dressmaker in Mandeville and wondered how prospective customers would react when they realized I had a hearing problem. I had to admit that I would be dealing with more sophisticated clients than at home. My customers in the rural district of St. Elizabeth were all local girls whom I had known all my life. But I told myself that I couldn't afford to fail. I couldn't afford to go back to my family in defeat. I knew that Dad and Grandma really expected me to fail; they had always said that I could never be successful anywhere else. So I realized that this was my one opportunity to prove to them that I could stand on my own two feet.

About a month after I had settled in Mandeville, I went back home to visit Grandma and Uncle Reggie and to pick up my fourteen-year-old sister, Juliet, who wanted to stay with me in Mandeville. Like me, Juliet seemed attracted to the bustling life of the city, and I was only too happy to have her with me. Unfortunately, Juliet stayed only two weeks and was very sad when she had to return home after her mother became sick.

I knew little about interior decorating, so Mrs. Hudson helped me decorate and arrange my sewing office. She introduced me to some of her friends as well. Though I was intimidated by taking on such an enormous job in unfamiliar surroundings, I did my best to make the office look as professional as possible. I had just received my certificate from the dress designing school, and I hung it on the wall where everyone could see it when they entered the office. I also had a large billboard posted outside the shop.

I knew I had to overcome my fears about communicating with my new customers. But I also knew I had the dressmaking skill to please others. I didn't want customers to be put off by my less-than-perfect speech. One of my first customers was an English lady whose husband was the manager at a Barclay's Bank. She came into my office immaculately dressed, the picture of perfection. At first I was intimidated but I soon realized that she was very friendly and accommodating, and I felt relaxed with her. She told me that she had been in Jamaica for only six months and that she had been looking for a dressmaker. I was really surprised since there were so many dressmakers in Mandeville. She was very pleased with the two dresses I made for her, and she dropped in one day to introduce me to two of her friends. She told me she was getting many compliments on the dresses I made for her, and that she would be bringing some other friends to me.

I had been in Mandeville for nearly two months when Brother Hall invited me to a special dinner with his family. He was a building contractor with a beautiful home in the suburbs. I met his lovely wife and two beautiful daughters, Anne and Margaret, and some of their friends. I was really surprised that the girls were so friendly and easy to talk to. I was shy and didn't know what to expect, but the girls kept up a barrage of talk about fashion which made it easy for me. "I saw your sign," one of the girls said. "You are the new dressmaker in town." she extended her hand. "I am so happy to meet you! I have patterns for several dresses I would like you to sew for me."

Their warm greetings really cheered me. A few days later, they all came to my shop with samples of material. They wanted my advice, and they planned to buy enough material to make several dresses. I helped them select fashionable styles from two *Vogue* magazines. Two of the girls were students at a nearby college, and before long, I was the dressmaker for more than a dozen of their friends.

In the weeks that followed, many of my customers introduced their friends, and their friends in turn brought more friends. Apparently word of mouth was all the advertisement I needed. After four months in Mandeville, I knew I was on the road to success. Since my customers were mainly business professionals and foreigners doing business in Jamaica, I knew I needed a different approach to dressmaking from what I was accustomed to in the country. I wanted not only to please my customers but to keep them coming back. I knew that getting new customers was one thing, but keeping them was another.

Past experience had taught me that every woman has certain likes and dislikes in fashion. So, I had each new customer fill out a simple questionnaire about her fashion preferences. I kept a file for each customer and referred to it whenever I made a dress for that client. Many of my clients, I realized, loved to wear low-cut necklines and tight-fitting dresses, while others were more comfortable in loose-fitting dresses. With so much competition from other dressmakers, I wanted not only to be a good dressmaker; I wanted to be the best. Fortunately, my design course had taught me the importance of being familiar with the profile of each individual girl, and I made it my highest priority to bring out the best in each client by minimizing any flaws in her figure.

My hard work paid off handsomely. As my business grew, I became more confident. It was like living in a dream from which I never wanted to wake up. I felt that everything I had dreamed and hoped for back home had become a reality.

Many of my clients who later became my friends were also single career women in their twenties and thirties. I really admired them; they were always well dressed, articulate, and they seemed to have all the confidence in the world. To me, they seemed more free, happy and contented than most married women. I worried less about being single—I was enjoying my freedom and I wanted to keep it that way.

The only dark cloud on my horizon was my hearing problem. I was acutely aware of my voice. I did my best to explain my hearing problem to new customers, but I always felt a little uncomfortable when I talked about it. I was brought up with the belief that most hearing people were prejudiced against deafness, and I hoped they didn't think less of me. I was probably trying to disconnect myself from my hearing loss in such a way that others would see it as an unfortunate illness, something that had happened to me a long time ago when I was just a child. Perhaps I was hoping they would see the real me as a normal person beyond the deafness. It was a relief to realize that most people didn't seem to be bothered by the fact that I couldn't hear.

My first four months in Mandeville turned out to be one of the busiest and most rewarding times of my life. I was comfortable staying with the Hudson family and always had breakfast and dinner with them. Dinnertime was relaxing for all of us. We had so much to talk about—mostly about our day at work. But then, I realized that I was missing out on some of the conversation, so I wasn't surprised one evening after dinner when Mr. Hudson asked, "Have you ever worn a hearing aid?"

I told him I hadn't. I remembered the disappointing examination with Dr. Ainsley Dujon, and my father shouting at me and telling me how stupid I was.

"I was almost eight years old when I lost my hearing," I told Mr. Hudson. "But I never found out what caused my hearing loss, and I never had my hearing tested."

By then everyone was looking at me in shocked disbelief. "You were just a child!" Mr. Hudson said. "Your parents should have taken you to have your hearing tested."

"My parents didn't believe any doctor could help me," I said defensively.

"It's really a pity your father didn't do anything. He could at least have taken you to a specialist." Mr. Hudson was silent for a minute. "You just can't go on living like this. You should try to get whatever help is possible. Have you ever heard of Dr. Kenneth McNeil? He is a very good ear specialist. I could make an appointment for you to go in and see him."

I had often heard of Dr. Kenneth McNeil. He was one of the most prominent ear, nose, and throat specialists on the island of Jamaica. He was also a prominent member of the Jamaica House of Representatives, and was best known as a politician.

About a month later I was in Dr. McNeil's office, face to face with this wonderful man about whom I had heard so much. He led me into a sound booth and gave me a battery of tests. Although the sounds I was hearing were confusing and different from anything I could remember during my hearing days, it gave me hope. When the test was over, he told me that I had some hearing in my left ear, but that I was profoundly deaf in my right ear. "If you had been wearing a hearing aid when you first lost your hearing, you could have adjusted very well to sounds," he said. He glanced at the sheet of paper in his hand. "It's more than twenty years since you lost your hearing. It is not going to be easy. The longer you wait, the harder it is for you to recognize speech and sounds. Since you have been without hearing for so long, I would recommend that you try speech and hearing therapy along with this hearing aid."

He held up something about the size of a pack of cigarettes with a long cord attached to it. "I am loaning you this hearing aid to see how well it works. It's free for thirty days. You can listen to normal conversations in the home. But don't wear it on the street. Sudden noise could be too much for you."

Although I was a bit disappointed that the hearing aid was so big, I didn't want to complain. I was hoping for one of those smaller models that could fit behind my ear. But I realized I had no choice, and figured that it was better than nothing.

When Mr. Hudson picked me up that evening for the trip back to Mandeville, I was so excited and grateful, I couldn't find words to thank him enough for all he had done for me. I had been with him and his family for barely three months, and he had done something my father would never have done for me.

It was late when we arrived in Mandeville so I went straight to bed. I had missed a day's work and I knew I had a lot of catching up to do the next day. Saturday was always a very busy day for me. I worked all day and throughout the night on Saturday, trying to meet a deadline.

On Sunday morning, I was very tired, so I called Brother Hall, my pastor who always picked me up for church every Sunday, to let him know that I would not be attending church that morning.

With everyone away at church, I looked out the window. It was a clear and beautiful day. I decided to put on my hearing aid and go for a walk along the quiet street. I sat on the steps outside my room and attached the hearing aid to my ear. The moment I flipped the switch, the whole world came alive with sounds. I didn't know where the sounds were coming from, so I glanced inside the open door. My eyes caught sight of the radio with its digital light blinking. I sat there listening for a while; suddenly I realized that someone was talking on the radio and I didn't recognize a single word—everything sounded funny and squeaky. Suddenly the sound changed and I was enveloped in a world of music. A cool breeze had come up, I closed my eyes and let the air and the music wash over me. My first reentry into the world of sound and music was thrilling and I felt exhilarated.

On Monday, I decided to wear the hearing aid to work. It was pretty bulky and much too obvious, and I was painfully aware of the stigma attached to deafness, so I was uncomfortable wearing the hearing aid in public. I sewed a patch-pocket into my work jacket to hide the bulky aid. Once I switched on the hearing aid, I was in for a rude awakening. I was completely unprepared for all the noise and confusion. It was embarrassing to realize that customers often talked to me when I wasn't looking. The hearing aid also picked up every sound around me. Everything sounded unreal, totally unlike anything I could remember from my hearing days. Even the voices of those around me sounded squeaky and funny.

At the same time, I was deliriously happy that I was able to hear again after more than twenty years. It seemed like everyone around me was talking and asking questions when I wasn't looking. I couldn't remember a time in my life when people talked so much. By the end of the day I felt fatigued from the strain of concentrating on both listening and lip-reading. The first week, I couldn't wait to get home and pull the hearing aid from my ear at the end of the day. I longed for complete peace and silence. I now understand why many deaf people refuse to wear hearing aids. For many of them, sound has no value, it is simply noise. And hearing noise is not going to help beyond alerting them to very few things.

I was disappointed that I was still unable to understand speech with the hearing aid. But it had become invaluable when I was out with friends. It helped me to know when background noise was going on so I could adjust my voice accordingly. I realized that many times I was unaware of background noise, and I was ashamed to realize that I was constantly blaming others for not responding to me when I might have been speaking too softly. The hearing aid helped me to adjust my voice to the volume of sounds or background noise and avoid this problem.

I had hoped to enroll in a speech-and-hearing class in Mandeville, but none was available. I wished I could relax and have a nice easy chat with my friends without having to watch their lips but that was not to be. After a month of wearing the hearing aid I was positive I wanted to keep it. I hadn't realized how much I was missing or that people were always talking to me when I wasn't looking. I was embarrassing to discover how often I failed to respond to people because I didn't hear them. I realized how annoying it is to talk to someone who does not respond. I now understood why my family and friends back home always touched me to get my attention, and I was aware that strangers might be too uncomfortable to touch me if I did not respond to them. They might think I was ignoring them.

Now that I was hearing sounds I had not heard in more than twenty-two years, I enjoy listening mostly to music on the radio. It took me some months to recognize the difference between the ringing of the telephone and the doorbell. Still, I found that the hearing aid was not as reliable as some people think. In a crowd, it amplified all kinds of sounds making everything more confusing than before.

Slowly I began to recognize the sound of people's voices, but I still could not recognize speech. I learned to recognize the difference in people's voice, and the sounds of their footsteps. And I remember the first time I went to the bathroom and flushed the toilet, the noise was so loud, I couldn't believe all the noise the water made!

Living in Mandeville opened up a world of opportunity I never knew existed for me. It seemed that everything my family had said was impossible for me to do was now possible. My business, and my confidence in myself, continued to grow. I marveled at how easy it was for me to make friends.

Driving a car was something I had never dared think was possible, and it came as a surprise one day when Mr. Hudson asked, "Would you like to drive a car?"

"Me?" I exclaimed, thinking he must be kidding. "Deaf people can't drive."

"Why not?" he asked. I shrugged my shoulders. "Well," he said. "I know several deaf drivers."

"Maybe they are not really deaf," I said.

"Well," Mr. Hudson said, "I am talking about some Americans who are sign-language teachers. They work just down the road from my shop." He went on talking. "They drive cars and vans and they don't seem to have any problem."

I found it hard to believe, so I said, "Are you sure they are really deaf? Maybe they are just sign-language teachers."

He then told me of a deaf couple who visited his shop almost every week, with their two kids as interpreters, and he promised. "Next time they visit I will let you know."

About a week later, Mr. Hudson rushed upstairs to tell me that the deaf couple was downstairs in his shop. I glanced out the window, eager to see what kind of vehicle they were driving. Parked close to the shop was a big white van, with a big red heart painted on the side. I could see the words in bold black capital letters, "Have a heart, help the deaf." I dropped what I was doing and rushed downstairs, anxious to meet the couple. As I approached the young couple to say "Hi," two young girls greeted me. The elder of the two, who, I figured, must have been around twelve years old, stepped forward and said politely, "May I interpret for you? My parents only use sign language."

"That's perfect with me," I said. "I can't hear but I can lip-read." I told the girls that I just wanted to meet their parents. While I spoke directly to the parents, the two girls kept signing and interpreting everything I said. I watched in amazement at the way they communicated with each other. The conversation between the parents and their daughters flowed easily and without any guesswork. It was my first real contact with anyone who used sign language, and I couldn't figure out a single word. I wanted to know how they understood each other so well. Unlike lipreading, there is no guesswork with sign language, and I was very impressed. They were a beautiful, intelligent young couple who looked so confident you wouldn't know they had a hearing problem. I could tell they were a wonderful family. And I was very glad I was able to meet them.

During my time in Mandeville, I took a weekend off to attend an inter-denominational convention. I shared a kitchen there with a friendly lady, Miss Daisy. We always found a lot to talk about when we were together. But then, one morning I got up early and went into the kitchen to get a cup of tea. Miss Daisy was standing over the sink with her back turned to me. "Morning, Miss Daisy," I said as I walked into the kitchen, but she didn't respond. The second morning it was the same; by then, I was beginning to wonder why she didn't respond. I thought that she was avoiding me. Imagine my surprise when we got together later that morning and she asked, "Did you know that I have a hearing problem?"

"Really?" I responded. "I wasn't aware you had a hearing problem, you showed no sign of it."

She talked about all the problems she had to face in a world geared for those who could hear. It opened my eyes to the fact that I was in the same situation with hearing people, especially those who didn't know I had a hearing disability.

It is easy to misjudge someone who have a hearing problem. I was reminded of the day I was on a bus, going to Kingston. The lady sitting next to me stuck up a lively conversation that went on for several minutes. As I glanced at a magazine I saw a questioning look on her face. Thinking she might have said something to me when I wasn't looking, I asked "Did you say something?" She nodded, so rather than have her think I was selfish, I said, "I am sorry, but I have a hearing problem." She looked at me as if I had evaporated; without saying a word, she walked over to a different seat. It really hurt when people acted so indifferent. Fortunately, most people are not like that.

CHAPTER 8

Out on a Limb

IN FEBRUARY, 1967, Mr. Hudson, decided to rent his home to the Kaiser Bauxite Company, and take up residence in the rooms above the shop where I was working. I had already made plans to move out and rent an apartment in Kingston with two of my cousins. I had been with the Hudson's for a little over a year. I had gotten to like the family so much, I never wanted to leave. But when I left, I knew I was wiser, and more mature than when I first came to live with them. I came away with a lot of respect and admiration for this wonderful family I had the good fortune to meet. My one year in Mandeville was one of the happiest times of my life.

When I moved to Kingston my life changed dramatically. I shared a two-room apartment on Kings House Road in Barbican with my cousins, Dell and Maxine. Life in Kingston was very different from my comfortable life in Mandeville. The high cost of the rent and utilities meant that I couldn't afford to live alone in the city.

Once I had settled in Kingston, however, I realized that I had the freedom I had always longed for. It was easy to get around the city using busses and taxis, and I took advantage of many new opportunities. Eager to improve my hearing and speech, I wanted to find a speech therapist right away.

Armed with my hearing aid, I took a cab to the Jamaica Association for the Deaf. It was the only place I could think of going for help. I knew I couldn't afford to pay a private speech therapist. I had contacted several of them and they all charged by the hour and the cost was extravagant.

I was apprehensive when I arrived at the Jamaica Association for the Deaf, not knowing what to expect. My interviewer, a pretty young girl from America, was friendly and easy to talk to, though, and I soon found myself relaxing.

"You can call me Rita," she said during the interview. "It's short for Margarita."

After the interview she asked, "Where did you learn to lip-read so well?"

I told her I had learned it naturally, mainly because I grew up with hearing playmates. "You speak very well," she went on, "and you are very good at lipreading. Very few people can lip-read as well as you do." I was thrilled to "hear" such wonderful words coming from the lips of someone who was a speech expert. It really boosted my confidence, and I promptly signed up for a six week speech therapy session.

I was assigned to a class with ten elderly ladies, all of whom had recently lost their hearing. At first I didn't understand why they wanted to learn lipreading especially so late in life. But during a conversation with several of them, I learned that they were unable to understand speech with their hearing aids.

"I am losing my family," one of them told me. "My grandchildren have given up trying to talk to me." My heart went out to her. I could understand the pain she felt and realized that the only way she could communicate with her family was to learn to read their lips.

After attending the second session, I realized I was the only one in the class who could easily communicate with Rita. We spent a lot of time discussing ways to help the others to understand lip-reading.

One day, Rita said to me, "I am teaching sign language tomorrow morning to a group of small children. I have a young mother in my class who is so heartbroken. She just found out that her five-year-old daughter is deaf and is not responding to a hearing aid. Elometer," she begged, "could you come in one day and speak to her for me? She is heartbroken, and nothing I say can ease her pain."

"But what could I possible do to help?"

"I think if she sees how well you turned out despite everything it may give her some hope for her daughter," Rita replied.

A week later, I arrived at the Jamaica Association for the Deaf a little early and was directed to the receptionist's room. There was a young lady sitting alone at a table. Thinking that she might be the lady I was supposed to meet, I introduced myself. "Hi, I am Elometer," I said extending my hand. "Are you waiting for someone?"

"No" she answered. She looked at her watch. "My daughter is attending sign language classes here. It starts in about thirty minutes."

As I took my seat on the other side of the table, I noticed a little girl sitting alone in a corner of the room busily playing with a doll. She was a beautiful child whose smooth skin and neatly braided hair showed the care and love of a mother. "Is that your daughter?" I asked.

She nodded. "Yes."

"She is very pretty. How old is she?" I asked.

"She is five." She went on to tell me how she had found out the month before that her daughter was profoundly deaf and would not be able to wear a hearing aid. Tears welled up in her eyes as she told me of her agony when the audiologist broke the news to her.

"I am sorry," I said, "but many deaf children turn out better than expected. Your daughter is very pretty and looks very intelligent."

I could see the agony on her face as she said, "She was born deaf. The audiologist told me she will not be able to speak, that only sign language can help her to communicate."

"Don't give up hope," I said. Hoping to help her, I added. "Many deaf children learn to speak. I am one of them."

She looked keenly into my face as if searching for something, and I could see the puzzled look on her face. "But you are not really deaf, are you?" she asked.

"Yes," I said. I still couldn't bring myself to say. "I am deaf."

"Then how can you understand what I am saying if you are not hearing me."

"Actually," I said, "I am not hearing a word you are saying. I am just reading your lips."

A look of surprise came over her face. "I can't believe this. I have never met anyone who can lip-read."

I smiled. "You met me, and you might have met and spoken to others without knowing they were deaf."

We talked for a few more minutes. When I said goodbye, she held onto my hand as if not wanting to let go. "I am really glad I met you. I can't thank you enough. You have given me so much to hope for."

I never saw the lady or her daughter again but I certainly hope I did something to give them hope.

The following week, I decided to pay a visit to one of the sign language classes that Rita was teaching. I wanted to understand how the children could learn a language that seemed so complex and confusing. What I saw convinced me that the kids were very happy learning to communicate with their hands. From that day on, I had a burning desire to help those kids and one of the first things I did was donate my hearing aid to the

Jamaica Association for the Deaf. I figured if the hearing aid could help one child to hear it would mean the world to him or her.

All the way home on the bus that day, I kept thinking about those children, some of them barely four years old. I couldn't understand why they were teaching them to communicate with their hands. *Why not teach them to talk instead?* I wondered to myself. And then the awful truth dawned on me: Many of those children were born without hearing and would never be able to hear the words they should reproduce. They would never know the true meaning of speech or sounds.

For the first time in my life, I realized how lucky I was to experience hearing and speech for the first seven years of my life. Yet, in a way, I was just like those children—living in a world where we see everything but never realizing that there are sounds around us all the time. I often wonder what would have happened to me if I had been born without hearing. *Would I be able to speak a language I had never heard?* It dawned on me that children born deaf are visually oriented and are more likely to respond to the things they can see, touch, and feel. This is one of the mysteries of sign language. Sign language is a true visual language. Unlike lipreading, which requires a lot of guesswork because a large percentage of the words we speak are invisible on the lips, sign language has no guesswork and is much easier for deaf children to learn.

We live in a society that judges others by the way they speak and by the way they write. Perhaps one of the biggest blind spots in our society is that many hearing people tend to see the inability of the deaf to communicate orally as a sign of disability. Most deaf people are very intelligent. The biggest barrier they face is not deafness but the public's view of them and their inability to communicate orally in a world geared for a hearing and speaking society.

At this stage in my life, I wished I could devote more time to helping others like me. But my business in Kingston wasn't doing as well as I had expected, and I needed to supplement my income. I began working as a private contractor to Joyce DeLisser. Joyce was one of the most prominent dress designers in Jamaica and a member of the Jamaican Fashion Export Guild Limited, a fashion export industry that was attracting some of the most popular dress designers on the island. My ambition was to become a member of the Guild, and I was lucky to have met Joyce at a time when she needed a garment cutter.

Best of all, it was a job that kept me feeling independent. Each week, I took a cab to Joyce's boutique to pick up rolls of fabric. I took them to my apartment and cut them into garments of various sizes. It was hard work, but I had come to realize that living in Kingston wasn't going to be easy. I had come to think of life in Kingston as "survival of the fittest," and I was struggling to be one of the fittest.

My persistence and hard work paid off. After a time, I was able to relax. The most important thing, however, was having the freedom to do what I wanted and go anywhere I wanted. Having a husband and children was the last thing on my mind. I was thirty years old and I had many friends and clients who were still single in their thirties. I really wanted to be like them, single and carefree. It felt that I had discovered what I really wanted to do with my life.

My roommates, Dell and Maxine, were both much younger than I was. They were working and helping to pay the rent on the apartment, but they were always talking about marriage, and I knew that my situation could change in a day. My roommates could move out, get married, or simply decide to go back to their parents. I worried that I could not afford to live alone in Kingston.

Fate has a way of making decisions for us, however. One hot summer day in August, a day like any other, I was in my room cutting some fabric when the assistant came in to tell me that someone was at the gate asking for me. I thought it was a customer, so I said, "let her in."

The assistant looked at me strangely. "It's a man."

Quickly, I parted the curtain and looked out the window. I couldn't believe my eyes. There was Linton Thomas, a guy I had been corresponding with for nearly three years. We had stopped writing to each other a year before, though, and I never expected to hear from him again. I didn't know how he had found me at my new address in Kingston.

My heart was pounding as I walked out to the gate. I didn't know what to do or say.

"You remember me don't you?" he asked.

I nodded. "I didn't know you were in Jamaica."

He flashed me a big smile. "I came up last week but I didn't know where to find you." He told me that he had called my last workplace in Mandeville and someone had given him my address.

I invited him into my apartment, and we talked for a long time. Suddenly, I remembered that I had to meet a deadline. I told him I was very busy.

"How about tomorrow?" he asked. I told him he could come back the next day when my roommates would be home "You can come back tomorrow and meet my cousin." I said

In the weeks that followed, Linton visited me very often, and in less than a month, he asked me to marry him. He was a good-looking guy, and I liked him in a way, but I just couldn't fall in love with him. I didn't feel any romantic attachment. It was more like a friend or a brother. Perhaps my problem was that, over the years, I had built up too many walls to protect myself from falling in love. Besides, I was on my own for the first time in my life—I was enjoying my freedom and I wasn't ready to give it up.

Two months later, though, something happened to make me see things differently. Early in October I took sick. I was in bed for two weeks with pain all over my body. I was so sick that I couldn't to do anything to help myself; Dell and Maxine were working, so there wasn't much they could do for me. I had been in bed for two days when Linton came to visit me. My illness had taken a turn for the worse that day, and I could hardly get out of bed. Linton just happened to be there at a time when I desperately needed help, and one of the first things he did was to rush out to the pharmacy to buy cold remedies and food.

I was deeply touched by his kindness, and I realized that I was beginning to like him very much. Yet I still saw married life as a burdensome responsibility, and I honestly didn't think I could cope with it. I had been subservient to my family for so many years that I was reluctant to give up my new freedom. I felt as if I had reached a crossroad and didn't know which way to turn. I knew that living with my roommates wasn't going to last for long, and I was beginning to wonder whether I truly wanted to remain single forever. Besides, I was scared of living alone.

I realized that Linton was a wonderful, caring person, and I had no doubt that he truly loved me, but somehow I kept telling myself not to rush into anything I might later regret. A major concern at the time was Linton's family. I had never met any of them and didn't know how they would react when they found out he was marrying a girl who couldn't hear. As for my family—I already knew how they would react. They would oppose my getting married to anyone.

I had a million questions constantly on my mind. I didn't know how I had lost my hearing. I didn't know whether it was the result of a fall or was caused by the medication the doctors had given me to save my life. I never found out what kind of illness I really had. I dreaded the possibility that my kids might end up inheriting my hearing loss. I also told myself that no child would want to grow up with a mother who couldn't hear. I feared that my children would grow up to resentment me. I knew I wouldn't be able to do many of the things that hearing mothers did. But my biggest heartbreak was the thought of having children whose little voices I would never be able to hear. I would never know when they woke up and cried. For the first time in my life, I had to acknowledge that my family might be right. They had instilled in me the belief that conventional marriage and childbearing was for hearing people and not for me. Perhaps they wanted to protect me from the heartbreak they thought I was likely to face.

I was still in this state of mind when Linton asked me to marry him for what must have been the hundredth time. I felt that I had no choice: I could never marry anyone. My heart went out to Linton, it was all too obvious that he really loved me, but there wasn't a thing I could do to make him understand why I couldn't get married to anyone.

But then, after he made the most heartrending plea to me, he said goodbye and told me he was returning to England. He did nothing of the kind, though. Instead, he went out and got so drunk that he almost died. When I saw him in that condition something inside me really went out to him. He was too nice a guy for me to hurt, and I really felt I should be there for him as he had been there for me when I was sick. I felt I had to give something back.

Once I had given Linton my word, I realized that there were many more obstacles to overcome than I had anticipated. I had to face the fact that his family might never accept me. The idea that I had never met any of them bothered me. But I knew there was no turning back for me. We were married by a Justice of the Peace, barely two weeks after I had accepted his proposal.

The night before our wedding, I couldn't sleep. I kept staring at the beaded pink dress I was planning to wear the next day. I wished I could have a real wedding like some of my friends. I wished I could make my own wedding dress. For a moment, I could envision myself walking down the aisle, all decked out in a traditional white chiffon gown. But when I thought of the audience who should be cheering me on, all I could see was disappointment on everyone's faces. I thought of my father and my grandmother, my brother Val, my sister Doris, my Aunt Lulu, all the people I loved and cared for, all the family who should be there for me. One by one my mind scanned the faces of all the family who would be shocked by my decision to marry a man they hadn't even met. *Would any of them be there for me?* I asked myself. My father's words came back to haunt me. "People like you have no right to marry." "How can you expect to bring children into the world? Who is going to teach them to talk? Who is going to care for them?" I buried my head in my hands and wept.

At ten o'clock on the morning of November seventh, while my roommates were at work, I slipped out of the house and into a waiting car that would take me to the registry office. It was the most difficult decision of my life and I was to re-live it for many years afterward. I was barely aware of the two unknown witnesses and the pastor telling Linton to move over to my other side. When it was my turn to repeat the wedding vows, I couldn't speak for a moment, but when I found my voice, I was able to continue to the end.

Back in the car, I was fighting back tears—tears that just wouldn't stop—tears of sadness at what I had done; tears of relief that I had had the courage, despite my doubts and fears, to go through with the marriage vows.

Sometimes I wish I were writing this story as a fiction story so that I could tell the whole heartbreaking story without worrying about hurting anyone in my family. I was certain that Linton and I truly loved each other and that our marriage could have been a very happy one. Sadly, the inability of my family to accept us made our situation very difficult.

My sudden marriage and move from the apartment I shared with Dell and Maxine put a temporary end to my career as a dress designer. I wasn't worried, though; I had the impression that Linton wanted to return to his job in England.

I was six weeks pregnant when I decided to visit my father with my new husband. Facing Dad after my sudden marriage was extraordinarily difficult for me because I knew he wasn't going to be happy, but I was already married and I was bringing a precious child into the world. At least I wasn't showing, so I didn't have to tell Dad about my pregnancy. My father had never met Linton, and I felt that it was time to introduce Linton to my family. But I was terribly disappointed by the reception I received. I had hoped that my family would be more receptive, instead of lecturing me. I could tell that Linton was terribly disappointed also. Although he said nothing, his silence spoke volumes.

Linton and I had barely settled down in a duplex apartment at DuPont Avenue when he began talking about buying a house in Kingston and going on a boat-fishing trip. I didn't understand why he no longer wanted to talk about going back to England. I still don't know what happened to make him decide to stay in Jamaica. I knew that he had just finished a navigation course and that he had fallen in love with the beach life in Jamaica, but I didn't know that he was crazy about the sea.

I was five months pregnant when Linton went away on his fishing trip. He promised he would be back within a week, so I wasn't really worried. Maxine was with me at the time. Maxine was a wonderful girl and we were the best of friends. My landlords, Mr. and Mrs. Montague and their two daughters, were a wonderful family, who I really got to like. They were warm and friendly people who made me feel at home. I also had two wonderful neighbors who lived across the street. With all these people around me, I wasn't really worried when Linton left for his fishing trip.

But, after a week had passed and Linton had not returned, I began to worry. By the end of the second week, I was frantic. It was so unlike him that I thought something must have happened to him. All kinds of possibilities went through my mind, and I began having nightmares. One night, I dreamed that he was dead and that I found his body washed up on the shore. I didn't know who to turn to for help. I didn't want to bother anyone with my problems so I didn't tell my family or my neighbors of my heartbreak. I wished Linton had some relatives that I could go to and find out what had happened to him. I didn't have a telephone, but I was able to make contact through my landlords. Although I tried to keep in touch with my family by letters, they never replied.

While Linton was away, I decided to make the down payment on the house he wanted to buy. It was my last chance to secure the deal, and I couldn't afford to let it go. I had every confidence that once Linton returned, my worries and financial problems would be a thing of the past. I had never been in dire need of money in all my working life. Whenever I had needed money, it had always turned up. But after I had made the down payment on the house and paid the rent on the apartment, I realized I still had to pay my hospital and doctor fees. I was quickly running out of cash and wondered how I was going to survive. Worst of all, I was always sick and had no appetite, and I couldn't sleep at night.

After two months, Linton still had not returned. Faith and prayer were the only things that sustained me, but I hadn't given up hope. I thought that, if Linton were dead, I would have somehow gotten the news.

My only relative who stayed in touch with me was my cousin Dell. I wasn't happy with the way my family reacted to my marriage.

I hadn't realized that the constant worrying was affecting my health until I visited the hospital. My obstetrician, Dr. C. Wilkins at Andrews Memorial Hospital, called me into his office. "Mrs. Thomas," he said, "I am very concerned about you. You are not gaining any weight. Are you eating properly?"

I didn't know how to tell him of the emotional turmoil and financial hardship I was going through.

"Have your husband call me tomorrow," Dr. Wilkins said. "It's very important for you to start gaining weight."

"He went on some boating trip," I said. "He hasn't been back for a while."

"I want you to bring your husband with you the next time you visit," Dr. Wilkins insisted.

When I visited the doctor on my next appointment, a month later, Linton still had not returned. I had to tell Dr. Wilkins that he was still away. It was obvious that the doctor did not believe me; perhaps he thought I didn't have a husband. He asked,

"How could your husband be on a boat trip for so long?" I simply shrugged my shoulders; there were nothing I could say

I gave birth before I was due, a result of the stress and worries. I was working on a dress for an important customer who happened to be one of my neighbors when I felt the first contraction. Five minutes later, I felt it again. I was frightened and didn't know what to do. Maxine was at work, so I got up and walked over to my next-door neighbor's place— she was also one of my customers and also happened to be a registered nurse. Lucky for me she was at home. She took my pulse, waited a few minutes, and confirmed that I was in labor. After she called a cab, I went back to my apartment to collect my things. The pains were not as bad as I had expected. My biggest concern was for my baby. In the hospital, I was in labor for three days, and I felt sure something had to be wrong. I wanted my baby to born healthy. Later, when the nurse handed me my sleeping little son and I gazed at him for the first time, I felt a happiness I had never felt before.

My son Mark was born premature, he was a tiny little thing, but perfect in every way. For the first time in my life I really wanted to live. I wanted to be there every moment for my son. I was definitely prepared, knowing I would never hear his little voice, but I told myself that I would be there for him whenever he needed me. I wished I had the money to buy a new hearing aid. It was distressing to know that without a hearing aid would never know when my son woke up and cried. In the days that followed, I realized that Mark had perfect hearing, and I realized how blessed I was. He was such a beautiful baby. I had much to thank God for.

Once I was home from the hospital with my baby son, I vowed that I would never forgive Linton, if I ever saw him again. But five days later he turned up, very thin and badly sunburned. I hardly recognized him. The moment I saw him in that condition I couldn't help but forgive him. He told me that his boat had sunk somewhere off the Keys in the Caribbean waters. He said that he and the others had survived by eating fish and other food they managed to get on the island. I knew then that I loved him enough to forgive him.

In August 1968 we moved into our new home, but with the awful realization that we might not be able to pay the mortgage. I didn't know that Linton had spent all of his savings on the boat that sank. I didn't even know where our next meal was coming from. Somehow, Linton sold whatever could be sold and went back to his job in England. I stayed behind to take care of things.

Luckily, I still had a few customers and was able to earn some much-needed money. But I knew that if I was going to do my job as a seamstress, I would have to hire someone to help care for my son. My cousin Lora, Uncle Walter's daughter, came to my rescue. I couldn't have been happier— she was a wonderful girl, very quiet, honest and easy to get along with. I think I could have died of loneliness living alone. Having someone to communicate with really helped me, and Lora and I had so much to talk about. I really don't know how I could have managed without her.

Once Linton began working in England, he was able to send me a check every two weeks. My business in Kingston was doing much better, and it didn't take long for me to attract many of my neighbors as customers.

In fact, my first two customers were my next-door neighbors, Mrs. Enid Foreman and Mrs. Lillian Brown. Enid and Lillian became my best friends as well.

After three months, I was on my feet again and able to relax and enjoy my new home. The next seven months was pure bliss for me: I had fun decorating my home, but I never wanted to spend too much on high-priced furniture, since I was expecting to join my husband in England. God had blessed me so much and answered my prayers so wonderfully. I felt that my days of despair and uncertainty were over as long as I had my home and my job.

Once my papers at the British Embassy were processed, I went to a booking agent and booked a flight to England. In March 1969, I left Jamaica to start a new life with my nine–month-old son. I thought I could handle things on my own. But when we landed at Heathrow Airport in London, and other passengers exited the plane, I should have asked for information. Instead I relied on the information board, which was a mistake. I realized that other passengers were turning their heads to hear an announcement. Too late, I realized that we were changing planes and most of the passengers had left. I missed the connecting flight and had to pay another airfare and wait another five hours. Finally, I boarded a plane to Birmingham Airport where Linton was waiting for me. I learned a lesson the hard way: don't be afraid to ask for help.

CHAPTER 9

England: The Migration

A s our plane taxied to a halt at Birmingham Airport, I realized that everyone was rushing to get out. I decided to take my time. I had two bags on one shoulder and a baby in my arms. Once I was on the ground, I felt the bitter biting cold. I wrapped the blanket around my little son as I struggled to keep up with the other travelers.

The airport terminal was crowded with people hustling back and forth. Out of the throng of people, I spotted my husband and my sister Doris walking toward me. Seeing my sister was the most wonderful surprise—I wasn't expecting her, and it really cheered me up. We had not lived together since our mother died, but I had always felt close to my sister. I hadn't seen her since she had left Jamaica for England more than eleven years earlier. As we drove out of the city, I was fascinated by the tall, stately buildings and the tall, leafless trees. It was strange to see so many trees all covered in white and without leaves. I had read many stories about Britain and other European countries, and I knew that the trees shed their leaves in the winter. But I had not expected to see anything so beautiful. With the snow on the ground, the city looked like a wonderland—something I had read about only in fairy tales.

Doris and her husband, Sydney, had four beautiful children: three girls and a boy. I was really happy to meet my three nieces, Barbara, Maureen, Diana, and my nephew, Gordon. I stayed with my sister and her family for a week in West Bromwich before joining my husband in Stoke-on-Trent where he was working. Linton must have realized how much I enjoyed staying with Doris and her family because, when he was offered a job in West Bromwich, he told me that we could stay there until we got our own place. I was very happy with the arrangement, but the most important thing for me was getting to know my nieces and nephew. They were sweet little kids and were a godsend for my young son. Things might have been much different if I hadn't gotten to know them so well. We became and remain a close-knit family.

Less than two months after I arrived in England, I realized I was pregnant again. As with my first pregnancy, I was taken by surprise. This time I felt more confident that things would be better for me the second time around—I wouldn't have to go through all the hardship, loneliness, and emotional turmoil of my first pregnancy. This time, I would be surrounded by family who loved me. Having two children was all I wanted: a boy and a girl. This time, I hoped for a girl. I fantasized that my children would take care of each other. Mark, as the older brother, would take care of his little sister; his little sister would always be there for him. That's the way I saw it, that's the way I hoped it would be.

I decided to stay at my sister's until after my baby, Anne-Marie Elizabeth, was born. She was a beautiful baby girl, to me, the most perfect baby I had ever seen. I was getting lots of compliment from everyone in the maternity ward about how beautiful my baby was. A month after Anne was born I purchased a hearing aid. Although I was unable to recognize speech with the aid, I wanted to keep it, because I realized that with it, I could hear when my kids woke up and cried.

My happiness was now complete: I had two wonderful children. They were my whole life, and I lavished all my attention on them. Maybe I was overprotective but I couldn't help it. I was happy and thankful to God, and I felt truly blessed.

Things were going very well for us. In November 1970, we went to visit Linton's brothers in Stoke-on-Trent. We stayed with Linton's brother Phillip and his wife, Margaret, a wonderful family with a young son. We visited another brother, Simon, the following day. Unfortunately, Simon's wife, Daphne, was not at home and I did not meet her until some years later. The following year we went to London to visit Linton's nephew, Louis, his niece Lorna, and their mother. It was wonderful to have met Linton's family and to receive such a warm welcome from all of them. We have all kept in touch ever since.

I was still staying with my sister. Although they told me I could stay for as long as I wanted. The problem was that there was only one spare room and it was much too small for the four of us. I wanted to start looking for a place of our own, but Linton would have none of it, and I could never understand why.

Although, I was still struggling to understand speech with the hearing aid, and still wanted to keep it. I wasn't getting any encouragement to keep it, though, I finally bowed to pressure from family and friends and finally gave it up. I was soon to regret that decision when Mark, my son, fell and I didn't hear him crying. It happened very suddenly. I just turned around and there he was lying on the ground, a cut on his forehead, crying, "Mommy, Mommy," and reaching out for me. I know that if I had kept the hearing aid I would have responded to his cries much sooner.

With my kids growing up so fast and asking lots of questions, I knew I had to be there for them. Even before my kids were two years old, they seemed to understand that I had a hearing loss, and that they had to touch me when they needed my attention. I will never forget the first time that

Mark, then only four years old, asked me why I couldn't hear. It was a cold and rainy winter night. Mark and Anne had come down with the flu. I put them to bed early, but it was late, past their bedtime, when they finally fell asleep. Worried and unable to sleep myself, I tiptoed downstairs to the kitchen to get a cup of tea. I was curled up in a chair with all the lights off to sip my tea. After a while I dozed off, and the next thing I knew, two little hands were tugging at my nightdress. It was Mark. I switched on the light. I picked up my son and hugged him to me. I felt the beating of his little heart against my chest. Mark was crying and I realized how frightened he was. It broke my heart knowing that my little son had come down the dark stairs crying and searching for me. After his crying subsided I said, "Baby, I am sorry, Mommy didn't hear you."

He lifted his head from my shoulder and stared curiously into my face. "Mommy, why can't you hear?"

I choked up, wondering how to explain my hearing loss to a four-year-old. "Don't worry, baby, Mommy will always be there for you," I told him. I was really relieved that Anne was safely asleep in her cot upstairs.

After I had put Mark back to bed, I lay in the dark, thinking about my children. I prayed that God would give me the opportunity to take care of them. But I often questioned my decision to have children. I was aware that my kids missed out on much in their young lives because they had a mother who couldn't hear. I worried that I might not be able to take them to places of entertainment. I hoped my kids would grow up to love and respect me, the way children love their hearing mothers. I hoped they would not grow up to be ashamed of me, though I knew that many children become angry or embarrassed around their parents.

After living with sister for nearly two years, I was desperate to have a place of my own. I realized that Linton was never going to do anything about getting a place for us. He talked continually about going back to Jamaica, where he could be out on the open sea. I never wanted to go back to Jamaica. To me, it was really distressing that he had fallen in love with the beach life in Jamaica, and there was nothing I could do about it.

To make matters worse, Linton was working the night shift at his job, and I was alone with the kids. Unlike hearing mothers, I couldn't relax and close my eyes after putting the kids to bed. I was afraid that they would wake up and start crying. I also knew that Linton wasn't getting enough sleep during the day with two small children running around. He became irritable when the kids played in the room.

When Mark was just over three years old, I enrolled him in a preschool, which gave him a place to play. When Mark was not at school, I often took the kids out to the park, but that was only possible during the spring and summer months. Once winter set in, there was no place to go. I felt cooped up in the little room day after day and had frequent headaches and began gaining weight.

Linton began insisting that I return to Jamaica and resume my career as a dress designer, but I resisted. I wanted my kids to grow up in England. My first priority was for the welfare of my children. I wanted them to get a good education and live a comfortable life in England. I had put my career on the back burner after my children were born. I also thought that, if I went back to dress designing in Jamaica, I would have to hire someone to take care of the kids, and I wanted to take care of them myself.

Around this time, I read about housing assistance in the local news and decided to seek help from the City Council of West Bromwich. Linton and I went for a half-hour interview and were put on a waiting list. After six months, a lady came out to interview us. Though Linton was not at home with me when she arrived, the meeting went well. Afterward, I was given a tour of a new three-bedroom house. I liked it instantly. It had everything we needed, and the weekly rental was reasonable. I knew we could easily afford to pay for it, so I signed up for it. I was told the house would be available in three weeks.

I could hardly wait to break the news to Linton. I thought of all the wonderful things we could do together as a family in our own home. I was certain that Linton would be happy to know we were getting a three-bedroom house. I had always wanted a home for my family. I felt it would bring my husband and me closer together. Best of all, the kids would have their own room and a place to play, and Linton would be able to sleep, undisturbed, during the day.

Linton arrived just as the lady who had interviewed me was about to leave. I was so sure he would be happy to know that we were getting place of our own, and at such a low rent, but I was in for a shock.

"Who is going to buy the furniture for that house?" he demanded. "You don't even have a job and we don't need a house." Turning to the lady, he pointed at me and said. "She is going back to Jamaica."

I stood there in stunned silence. I couldn't understand what had happened to make Linton so angry. In all the months we were on the waiting list, he never discouraged me, and all that time I thought he wanted a house too. I tried to think of something that might have upset him but I couldn't think of a single thing.

I watched helplessly as the lady said goodbye and walked away, and a feeling of despair washed over me. Just a few minutes before I had been happy and full of hope, now all my hopes had been dashed to the ground.

I became very depressed. I had pinned all my hopes on getting a place for the four of us, and now that hope had died. I soon realized that this was only the beginning of my troubles. Out of the blue, Linton dropped another bombshell.

"You are leaving for Jamaica in six weeks." he said, handing me a boat ticket.

I stared in disbelief at the ticket in my hands. "Why are you doing this to me?" was all I could manage to say, but I was close to tears. He had booked my fare on a passenger boat that was scheduled to sail from Southampton on September 4, 1973. The boat would take two weeks to reach Jamaica.

"Where am I supposed to stay in Jamaica?" I asked. "We don't have a house, have you forgotten our house is rented?"

"I don't care who you stay with. Go to anyone who will accept you," he shot back.

I told him I wasn't going, and swore that he couldn't force me to leave. "Well," he said defiantly "you can stay and I will go. You don't even work. Who is going to support you with two kids in England?"

I had had enough of his arguments and felt resigned to my fate.

"You are right. I will go. But nothing is ever going to be the same between us ever again."

Nevertheless, I spent the next six weeks pleading with him to reconsider.

I had six weeks to prepare for the trip back to Jamaica, and during those six weeks I finally took a hard look at myself. I didn't like what I saw. All my life, I had allowed myself to be manipulated. I had been stepped on too often by others. Now my husband was doing the same thing.

When I saw that there was nothing I could do. I knew I had to act fast. I would need someone to meet me at the pier when the ship docked. The only relative I could think of was my cousin Audley, so I wrote to him. He promptly wrote back, letting me know that he would be there for me. I still didn't know where I would be staying, so I wrote to Aunt Lulu. Once I had heard from Aunt Lulu I felt more confident. She was always like a mother to me and I knew I would be happy with her, but I didn't want to impose on her for too long. I wrote to the tenants in my house to let them know that I would be returning to Jamaica and would need my home within three months.

The day I said goodbye to my family and friends was heartbreaking. Many of my family and friends, had traveled to Southampton to see us off. My little daughter, Anne, only three years old, cried when we said goodbye to my sister Doris and my niece Barbara. She begged, "Don't go, Mommy." She seemed to know that we was really saying goodbye for good.

I had been in England for four years and six months. When I sailed for Jamaica with my two kids, I felt a mixture of sadness and relief. It was sad to say goodbye to my beloved family, but I was relieved to be getting away from a husband who seemed to want me out of his life. I felt that my marriage of barely six years was coming to a close.

My room on the ship was small and uncomfortable. It had only two small beds, and we had to share it with another woman, who occupied one of the beds. I had to sleep in the other bed with my two kids. We were on the bottom floor of the ship. The heat, and constant rolling of the ship, and the overpowering scent of the sea were unbearable. I felt as if I had landed in jail. The room had no window and we couldn't see anything except the walls. We spent most of our time on the deck, where the air was cool and comforting, and I was able to interact with other passengers. There I met a friendly group of Seventh Day Adventists, and I began attending group meeting with them. As a child, I had read many books published by Seventh Day Adventist authors, so I was familiar with the doctrine they represented and I understood the many Bible topics they discussed.

I had been on the ship for only three days when Anne took sick late one night. She was vomiting and I had to rush her to the only bathroom, which wasn't very close to my room. When I returned, I was shocked to find that my room door was wide open and the other woman, who had been in her bed when I left the room, was nowhere to be seen. I looked around the room and saw that my pillow was on the floor. It suddenly hit me that my wallet with all my money that I had tucked under my pillow was gone. I sat on my bed wondering what to do. Who could I contact at that time of night? The staff seemed to speak only Spanish. I felt lucky that the wallet contained only cash—I had locked my passport and other important papers in my suitcase, and I kept the keys on a chain around my neck. As I sat there wondering what to do, I remembered seeing a police box with information in English. I sat down and wrote a letter outlining how I had been robbed. I took the kids with me to the police box and dropped the letter in, then went back to my room and prayed as I never had in a long time. I didn't sleep that night and the woman never returned to the room.

It was a little too early for breakfast but I decided to get the kids ready and take them upstairs. I was about to lock the door when two uniformed men walked up to me. They spoke perfect English. After asking a few questions, one of them said, "We are here to take you to another room. Where are your suitcases?"

I gave them my two suitcases and followed them to a room upstairs. The room was bright, cool, and airy; there were two comfortable bunk beds with clean white covers, a wash basin, soap, lotion, and lots of clean towels. They explained to me that this would be my room for the duration of the trip.

After they left, I looked out the window and I could see the wonderful blue sky above and the matching blue waves bubbling along with the ship. I noticed that most of the passengers on the deck looked like tourists. They were very friendly and most of them spoke basic English. I learned later that most of them were from Venezuela and the Canary Islands. I should have felt happy getting such a comfortable room after the depressing heat in the basement, but the loss of all my money made me feel helpless.

The next day, as I sat at lunch, the captain, a tall sandy-haired man, handed me a large envelope. I opened it to find enough cash to replace most of the cash that was stolen. I was told that the captain had put out a collection for me, and I later learned that his office was just across from my room. One thing I knew, God was surely looking out for me, and He had heard my prayers. The comfort for me and the kids was more than I expected. The rest of our trip went like a breeze.

My cousin Audley was at the wharf waiting to greet us. When he drove us to his home, I was really surprised at how successful he had become. He was the manager of a bank and a very successful businessman in Kingston. He had built a beautiful home, complete with a swimming pool, in the exclusive suburb of Beverly Hills. I was really happy for him. He and his wife, Eula, were among the few family members I could rely on. I was also grateful to my Aunt Lulu for traveling all the way to Kingston to see what she could do for me and for letting me stay in her home for three long months while I waited for the tenants to leave my house. I don't know how I would have managed without her help. She was a wonderful person with a heart of gold. Aunt Lulu died several years ago, but her memory will always live with me.

Two weeks before Christmas, the tenants moved out of my home, and I moved in immediately. I was thrilled when my niece Audrey agreed to stay with me. She has done so much for me and the kids. It is hard to find someone as honest and hardworking, and I was glad that she stayed with me until I was ready to leave for the United States.

I had barely moved into my home and had not yet unpacked most of my things; I had only a few pieces of furniture and the house was in disarray when a burglar broke in. I had been warned about the high rate of crime in Kingston but I didn't think it would happen to me.

It was still pretty dark when I went to the bathroom that morning. I was sitting on the toilet, half asleep. I noticed that the bathroom door was moving slowly. I thought it was one of the kids, so I said, "Come in." The door continued to move very slowly. By then, I was thinking this was strange, but I said, "Come in, baby, Mommy's here."

Suddenly the door flew open, and before I knew what had happened, a man with a knife was standing over me. He pressed the knife against my throat and for a moment I thought I was going to faint. I could not believe that what I was seeing was real. It took me some time to make sense of what he was saying.

When I found my voice the first thing I managed to say was, "What do you want?"

He pressed the knife further. "You have money, don't you?" he held up the knife. "I don't want to use this," I watched as he wielded the knife. "I won't harm you or your family as long as I get that money." After what seemed like an eternity, he folded the knife, dropped it in his pocket, and said, "I am letting you out of here but if you set off an alarm I am going to kill you all." He then let me out of the bathroom.

I was shaking with fear. I thought of my niece and my little kids sleeping in their beds. I remembered that I had no cash in the house. I had been using a checkbook for all my purchases. I had to think fast. If I told him I had no money, he wouldn't believe me and he might become violent. I looked into his face pleading. He didn't look like a violent person. He was young, probably in his early twenties.

"My niece has the keys. I have to wake her." I said.

I started walking toward Audrey's room, but he held me back. "You can't go in there." He gripped my hand. "Remember what I told you, call her from here."

I stood in the doorway and called Audrey's name several times until she woke up. "Audrey," I said, "where did you put the keys?"

Audrey was rubbing her eyes and she looked confused I knew she didn't have the keys, and I didn't want to draw any suspicion so before she could answer. I went through all the rooms pretending to look for the keys. I rummaged through the things I had been unpacking. The guy followed me everywhere I went, and I pleaded with him. "I just moved here, I haven't unpacked yet," I said, hoping he would understand.

Suddenly, I had an idea. I had to get him out of the house, away from my family, before he did any harm to them. I remembered that the kitchen door leading to the carport would lock when it was slammed shut. I rushed through the kitchen door hoping he would follow me out into the carport. He did. Once we were outside, I quickly slammed the door, knowing it would lock automatically and he would not be able to get back into the house to harm my family.

I really expected to be stabbed right there in the carport, so I rushed out of the carport toward the gate screaming, "Fire, fire, fire."

The guy looked at me as if I had gone mad, then he jumped over the gate and made a quick dash down the street. I sagged against the gate as relief washed over me, barely aware that I was surrounded by people asking, "Where is the fire?"

"There is no fire," I managed to say. "Someone was in my house threatening me with a knife." I turned around and said to Audrey, "Please hurry, call the police."

"How did he get in?" everyone was asking.

My whole body was shaking like a leaf. I hadn't even thought about how he had gotten into the house.

I walked into the house and immediately checked on my kids. I was relieved to find them soundly asleep. I was still in the kids' room when one of the neighbors pulled me away to show me the broken window in one of the back bedrooms.

Later that day, my next-door neighbor came over to talk to me. She wanted to know how I had managed to get the robber out of my house without him harming me or my family. Audrey was also surprised that I was able to keep so calm. She said, "I am glad it wasn't me because I would have let out a scream! Aunt Nita, I didn't even know that a robber was in the house. I thought the guy was someone you knew because you were talking to him like a friend." She told me that the only time she suspected that something was wrong when she heard me screaming "Fire" outside.

My other neighbor told me that when she went back to her house, she realized that one of her windows at the back of her house was also broken. But the robber wasn't able to get in because she had burglar bars built inside all the windows. Most of the neighbors had become very friendly and they all wanted to know why I was calling "Fire" instead of calling for help. I told them that just two days before, I had read a leaflet about what to do in case of a burglary. The leaflet said that it was safer to call for fire because people are more willing to respond to a call for fire than a hold-up because the robber might have a gun.

I immediately contacted a workman who was working on a house nearby, and he was able to install a new window before the day was over. Two weeks later, my house was completely secured with burglar bars and I felt somewhat safer.

Next, I had to find a private school for Mark. The local public school, I was told, was beset by too many problems. Ann, not yet four years old, was too young to attend school, but she already knew the letters of the alphabet. I was lucky enough to find a private school for Mark near our house. It was a small school and I felt he would be much safer there than in the public school.

Late in February, I decided to start a dressmaking business in my home. But after five years of unemployment, I knew that starting a business that no longer had the same passion for me wasn't going to be easy. I had arrived in Kingston at a time when the city was torn by political unrest and a collapsing economy, and most of my former customers in Kingston had long since left Jamaica. I felt that I should be doing something useful, though, so I decided to convert the maid's room into a sewing room. I had a countertop installed in the center of the room as a cutting table, and I had wardrobe built with a full-length sliding mirror. It was like a small office and the perfect place to sew and fit my customers without interruption from the kids. But I still couldn't make up my mind. After several weeks of indecision, I posted a dressmaking sign out on my front lawn. I was really surprised at how easy it was to get customers. The money was good and it helped me to furnish my home nicely.

After a year, I had settled down and was content to make Jamaica my home. Both of my kids were doing well in school; I was independent; I had a home. I had moved on with my life and, although I didn't have a lot of money, I was able to buy the things I needed most. Linton and I kept in touch as if nothing had happened, and I was satisfied with that.

I had been in Jamaica for more than two years when my brother Val wrote, suggesting that he could get us a permanent visa for residence in the United States. At first, I didn't want to go. I had bought some of the best furniture I could afford and I was proud of my home. But I felt that this was an opportunity I couldn't afford to miss. To me, America was the land of opportunity, a place I had always associated with glamour, fashion, and movie stars. But the opportunity I saw was not for me, it was for my two children. Growing up in America, they could get a good education and live a comfortable life. I wasn't sure I could pay college education for two kids in Jamaica. On the other hand, I wondered where I would fit in. I didn't expect to get a job in America, and I had two small children to care for. My husband had his job in England and I had mine in Jamaica. Pulling up roots and moving to a country in which I never expected to succeed didn't make sense.

After a year, I began to see things differently. I thought about the opportunities my kids would have in America. By the middle of 1977, my immigration papers were approved, and I looked forward to a new life in America.

One big hurdle remained. Val wanted me to return to England to join my husband, so we could immigrate to the United States as a family. But I did not want to return to England. Linton and I had been living apart for almost five years when my visa was approved. For the past two years Linton and I agreed that he would keep his earnings in England because of the economic conditions in Jamaica. I knew that Linton wanted to make all of my decisions for me, but this was a decision he would never be able to make as long as I was living in Jamaica.

I let Val know that I was not going back to England. When my papers were approved, I wrote to Linton, letting him know that I was leaving for America. To my surprise, Linton promptly flew to Jamaica with the intention of getting me to stay there. But after nearly five years of separation, I had gotten used to my life, and I loved my freedom, and I wanted to hold on to it. When Linton saw that he could do nothing to stop me, he went ahead and got his papers ready to travel with us.

I had to decide what to do with my furniture. They was very expensive and I had spent more than four years paying for them. I wouldn't have brought such expensive furniture if I had known I would be leaving Jamaica. I knew that if I sold the furniture, I wouldn't get a fair price, so I decided to give it to my father as a gift.

Saying goodbye to Grandma, Dad, Aunt Lulu, and the rest of the family was hard. But I looked forward to seeing my brother Val, and I really felt that Val was lonely living all alone by himself for so long. We had always kept in touch, and as a family, I hoped we could help each other.

Once again, I put up my home for rent. I really didn't want to leave. I had put all my hopes and dreams into my home, and it was hard to leave all my good memories behind. We also left our sweet little cat, Timmy. Every time I see a cat that looks like Timmy, I want to cry. Our next-door neighbors, who had become close friends, loved cats and agreed to take Timmy into their home, so I knew he was in good hands.

CHAPTER 10

America: Home Sweet Home

I ARRIVED AT KENNEDY Airport on a cold winter day in January 1978, with my husband and two children at my side. As we waited for Val to arrive, I watched the bustling crowd. So this is what life in America is like, I told myself. It made me wonder if I would ever be able to succeed in America. I consoled myself with the thought that I was doing this for my kids' future. Despite my doubts and fears, I was happy to be in America. As a child, I had dreamed about living and working in New York City, the center of glamour and fashion. It was hard to believe that I was really in America.

Soon, I saw Val and my cousin Dell walking toward us. It was like a dream come true when they hugged us warmly and said the three most wonderful words: "Welcome to America."

The long drive to Val's apartment in Brooklyn was memorable. It was late at night, traffic was heavy, and the city was ablaze with lights. It was a small taste of how different life here would be. In the next two weeks, I learned to use the subway and to get around by myself. Val took a week off from his job to show us around the city and get us settled in his apartment on Sterling Street. A week later, he took me to Kings County Hospital for an audiogram and a new hearing aid. I had been wearing my old hearing aid on and off for more than four years. When I was fitted with the new hearing aid, it was like starting all over again. By then I had begun to understand the limitations of hearing aids. There was nothing new in my experience with the new one, which I found discouraging.

Less than two weeks after we arrived, Linton found his first job. That same week, we enrolled Mark in PS 161, a public school near our apartment. I would have preferred for both of my children to attend the same school, but I was advised to enroll Anne in St. Francis of Assisi because she was a brilliant student.

With my husband and brother away at work and my kids at school, the apartment became a lonely place, and I got restless. I really wanted to work but I also wanted to be there for my kids. They were still young and needed supervision; I didn't want them to be walking to and from school on their own. I was not willing to depend on Linton and what he was earning, and he was away too often from home.

Within a year, we moved from Val's apartment to another apartment a few blocks away on Lefferts Avenue. I became good friends with two of our neighbors on Lefferts Avenue, Patricia (Pat) Rock and Kitty Leslie.

Being alone in the apartment was uncomfortable for me. Since I couldn't hear if someone was at the door, I made it a habit to look through the peephole very often. We were in a strange city where the crime rate was high, and I realized that I couldn't be too careful.

Mark, and Anne, had been attending school for only two weeks when, as usual, I was on the lookout for strange goings-on in the hallway. Val had warned me about the high rate of crimes in the city. Imagine my surprise one afternoon when I happened to look out the peephole and saw my seven-year-old daughter standing outside the door with the school guard. I quickly opened the door and picked up my daughter. "What happened?" I asked.

The young guy looked a bit perplexed. "She was standing outside in the snow," he told me. "She told me she was waiting for her mommy."

I shuddered. "Why was she out in the snow?" I asked. I didn't wait for an answer.

"Did you know the school closed at twelve today?" he asked.

Anne was clutching at me and crying, "Mommy, my feet hurt."

I thanked the guy, rushed inside, and pulled off her snowy boots. I wrapped her in a blanket. I was frantic with worry when she wouldn't stop crying, so I grabbed a hair dryer and began blowing hot air over the blanket, hoping the pain would go away more quickly. It seemed like an eternity before the pain subsided and she began to relax. "Mommy," she asked, "How did you knew we were at the door? We didn't even knock." I just hugged her close until she fell asleep, then I closed the door and walked out of the room. I felt the tears began to fall, but they were tears of thankfulness, knowing it was divine guidance that led me to the door just in time.

The next day, I went to the school to find out what had happened. The teacher admitted that she hadn't told me that the school would close at noon that day. Val went right back to the school and pulled Anne out of school; two days later we enrolled her in the local school with Mark.

The apartment was cold most of the time, so I often stopped at the library after dropping the kids off at school. I had a list of books I wanted to read, and while browsing, I also noticed three books on the subject of deafness. I saw that they had not been borrowed in more than two years so I decided to borrow all of them. They were very informative books on the subject of hearing loss, and I couldn't understand why no one was reading them. When I returned the books to the library, I decided to look for them six months later. It was very discouraging to see that none of the books had been borrowed from the date I had returned them.

Pat and I often went shopping together on weekends, and I soon learned to get around the city by myself. Pat was a pro when it came to shopping and she seemed to know New York City like the back of her hands. We always had fun together.

In the spring of 1980, I began looking for a job. I didn't have a typewriter or printer to do my resume, so Pat, who was working at a law firm at the time, offered to help. Kitty helped me get my first job at a dress manufacturing company in Brooklyn where she was working. I was lucky to get the job at P. Lamonica, a company that specialized mainly in designer dresses. The employees at P. Lamonica, was mostly Italians, very friendly and easy to work with. I loved the opportunity to work on so many glamorous dresses.

When I got my job, Linton had just lost his job. He was at home most of the time. I figured he would take care of the kids, leaving me free to work. There was a strike at the steel manufacturing company where Linton had been working, and the company eventually closed down. After being on unemployment for six months and rather than look for another job, Linton decided to go back to Jamaica. I don't think he ever wanted to stay in America. He always said that he could make a better living in Jamaica.

My job at P. Lamonica lasted only a year. When the company went out of business, I began working at Dalmer's, another dress manufacturing company in Manhattan. My job at Dalmer's was very interesting and offered experience working with various types of industrial sewing machines. I loved working with many types of fabrics. Many of the employees were European, mostly Italian, and they were very friendly and easy to get along with. Unfortunately, the job at Dalmer's was seasonal, and during the slow period we had to be on unemployment.

With my husband away in Jamaica and two children to take care of, I was desperate to find a job that could, at least, provide steady, year-round employment with health benefits.

In the summer of 1983, Linton came back to America. He had been away for a year, and I hoped that he had come back to stay. I was disappointed to learn that he was only visiting us for a week. I tried to persuade him to stay in America and help me with the kids. I hoped for us to be together as a family, working and saving, so that we could eventually buy our own home, raise our kids, and send them to college, but this was not to be. The day before Linton was due to leave for Jamaica, our apartment was robbed and we lost most of the things we had spent the past five years working to acquire.

I don't know how I would have survived those early years without Val's help. He believed in me and was always there for us; he was more of a father to my kids than their own father. In the spring of 1984, Val brought a four-bedroom house in Kendall Park, a New Jersey suburb not far from Princeton. He was working at Merrill Lynch on Wall Street in Manhattan, but his department was relocating to Princeton. He decided to relocate with his job. Meanwhile I didn't have a steady job, and had no husband and no means of paying the rent on my own with two teenage children to support. I felt very fortunate that Val wanted us to move into his new home with him.

Getting away from the apartment at Lefferts Avenue in Brooklyn was a tremendous relief for me. I had been living in fear ever since our apartment was robbed. Then, less than a month later, we had to exit the building late one night when there was a fire in one of the apartments on the ground floor. I dreaded what might happen next. Moving to the quiet suburb of Kendall Park was a welcome change from the overcrowded apartment in New York. Yet in a way I missed New York. I don't think anyone can live in New York without falling in love with the city, and I certainly left my heart there.

When we moved to New Jersey in April, 1984, I didn't anticipate the major commuting problem. I wished we had stayed in Brooklyn until the end of the school year. Mark and Anne, still had two months of schooling in New York before the summer. Anne was due to graduate from junior high at PS 161 in Brooklyn in June, and Mark would complete his first year of high school at Martin Luther King High School in Manhattan in June. The long commute between New York and New Jersey, a total of almost four hours a day, was difficult and stressful for all of us.

By the middle of June, with the kids out of school for the summer I was very relieved. Linton was back from Jamaica. But he was no longer the same healthy man he used to be—he was frail and thin, just a shadow of his former self. I was surprised that he wanted to stay and work; he didn't look healthy enough to work. I begged him to let me take him to a doctor but he stubbornly refused. He eventually got a job working with Wells Fargo in Manhattan.

In September 1984 with my children enrolled in South Brunswick High School, I had reason to be happy. We were now living in a private home and we felt safe and secure in the quiet neighborhood. I was still working in New York but, I didn't mind the long commute on the suburban bus to Manhattan. I relaxed, read, and slept during the ninety-minute ride and eventually even looked forward to it.

I was all wrapped up in my own world when I learned of my grandmother's death. She was ninety seven years old. I felt guilty that I hadn't been back to Jamaica to see her. Val and I had planned to celebrate her hundredth birthday in Jamaica, but she died just three years short of it.

The trip back to my old homestead brought back a lifetime of memories: Memories of Grandma and me as a little girl whose life was forever changed by her mother's death. Memories of the good times I had playing on the farm. Memories of the day I came home from the hospital to find a different world awaiting me. Memories of growing up in a world where I was different from other children. Memories of the day I said goodbye to Grandma for the last time and how brave she tried to appear.

On the day of the funeral, there were hundreds of cars all over the farm. It was very comforting that so many people came to show their respect. It seemed that "everyone" I grew up with was there, and the years had changed most of them. Out of the throng of people I could barely recognize my best friend Muriel as she walked toward me. She had cut her long auburn hair to shoulder length. She was still beautiful, but somehow her face looked different to me.

After the funeral, Dad, Val and some of my relatives decided to tour the farm, but I didn't feel like joining them.

"Would you mind if I go into the house and look around for a while?" I asked as they set off for the tour. The moment I stepped inside the house I wished I hadn't. The rooms were dark and dismal with every window and door closed, the air was stale, and it didn't look like the home I had once lived in. I walked down the hallway and made my way to Grandma's room, bracing myself for any emotion that might overcome me. I stood at the foot of her bed, trying to recapture some of the happy times we had, but there was none of the beauty and charm that had been there in the days when Grandma was still alive and vibrant.

I glanced over at the bed where Grandma had spent the last years of her life, and was overcome with guilt that I hadn't cared for her during her last days. I had carried that guilt with me ever since I left home. I kept remembering my father's words, that it was God's will for me to take care of Grandma until she died.

I dropped my bag at the foot of the bed, closed my eyes for a long time, and said a prayer. After a time my mind shifted to the present and the realization that if I had stayed with Grandma to the very end, I wouldn't have anywhere to live. I knew the home belonged to Uncle Everett and he was planning to sell it when Grandma died. I thanked God that I had a husband and two wonderful teenage children waiting for me back home in America. This was my destiny, I told myself. This was God's plan for me. I couldn't imagine my life without my husband and children. I picked up my bag and walked out into the bright sunshine. All the guilt I had carried with me all these years suddenly rolled off my shoulders. Grandma was at peace, and I was finally at peace with God, my conscience, and the world

Back from Jamaica, I realized that business at Dalmer's had slowed down and once again I was on unemployment. During a trip to the unemployment office in June, I learned that Marriott was building a grand new hotel, which was due to open on Broadway in August. I learned that a team from Marriott International would be at the unemployment office to interview prospective employees for work. Mr. Weitz, who worked at the unemployment office, informed me that Marriott was in the process of recruiting several seamstress for the opening of the hotel in August. When he outlined the wages and health benefits, including generous stocks options, I realized this was an ideal job for me and I made up my mind to do anything I could to get that job. Mr. Weitz encouraged me to bring my resume and sign up for an interview.

I knew very little about Marriott then, but I began to read everything I could find about the company. I learned that Marriott was a company that believed in loyalty, family, and promoting employees from within the company.

I really wanted to get into that employee-friendly company, but when I went for the first interview and saw so many younger girls, who all seemed well educated and who also sought the seamstress job, I didn't think I had a chance, especially when I found out that many of them were graduates of fashion schools in New York City. I had my diploma in fashion design and a resume showing my years of experience, and I hoped that that would be enough to help me get the job. I was even more disappointed when I read the four requirements for the job:

(1) Must be at least 18 years of age.
(2) Must have high school education.
(3) Must be able to answer the telephone upon 3 rings.
(4) Must be bilingual.

I knew I could only answer one of them: I was over 18 years old, but I was not bilingual, I could not answer the telephone, and I didn't have a high school education. If they questioned my education, I would just tell the truth. I figured I could safely say that I had high–school level training at home. As it turned out, they did not ask me about my high school education.

I was sure I would be out by the first interview, so I was surprised when I was given a date for a second interview. My third interview, with someone from the human resources department at Marriott, lasted a half-hour. I was nervous but I tried not to show it. I dreaded the possibility that I might misinterpret some words. To my surprise, the interviewer was very nice. After the interview he said. "We are looking for someone with at least two years of experience in the garment industry who can handle the various types of sewing machines. I can see from your resume that you have been working for three years with a company that makes designer dresses."

After meeting the director of services, Sue Bamberger, and her assistant, Punch Schnietz, I began to feel more confident. After my fourth interview, I was told that I would have to take a polygraph test. I knew nothing about polygraph tests or how they were administered, so I was a little discouraged when I realized that the tester would be asking the questions behind my back.

"I am not going to hear anything you say," I told him. "I have a hearing problem. I can only read your lips."

He was very friendly and accommodating. "I will make it very easy for you. Just answer yes or no to each question," he said, placing a sheet of paper before me. Using a pen, he stood behind me and pointed to each question he wanted me to answer. When the test was over, he told me, "You will hear from us within a week."

I got the call a few days later informing me that I had gotten the job. They promised to call me back to let me know when I would be scheduled to start work.

I had an idea where the hotel was located but I wasn't sure, so the following day I made a trip to Manhattan. As I walked toward 45th Street and Broadway, I expected to see a much smaller hotel building. Imagine my surprise and excitement as I gazed at the sign from the beautiful, towering building: "New York Marriott Marquis." I was out of breath. "This is a beautiful hotel," I whispered to myself. I decided I had to go inside and see for myself.

It was obvious from all the activity that there were a lot of work still to be done before the hotel could open. A manager with a walkie-talkie came toward me. "Are you looking for someone?" I told her I was a new employee who would be working at the hotel but didn't have a work schedule yet. "I just wanted to see the hotel." I said finally

"Would you like me to contact someone?" she asked. I realized that the telephones were not installed as yet, because she was using a walkie-talkie. I felt like a foolish intruder.

"Sue Bamberger, please," I blurted out.

I waited as she made the call. Turning to me she said, smiling. "Sue would like to see you. She is sending someone down for you."

Norma, a young Spanish girl, came toward me and held out her hands. "I am Sue's assistant. You can come with me, but we will have to walk upstairs—there is no elevator."

Sue told me that their first priority was to get the guest rooms ready for opening day and that they needed employees willing to help the housekeepers. If I was willing, I could start working right away.

I started working the next day. It was hard work but I am glad I did it. I got to meet so many nice people, and it helped to prepare me for the work ahead. I was one of the first to meet our first manager, Bill Cullen, a handsome twenty-three-year-old. It was his first job since leaving college, but he proved to be an efficient manager. Wise beyond his years, he was one of the most honest, hardworking people I have ever met. Under his management, I gained a lot of confidence. Fortunately, Bill was one of those rare people whose speech was so perfect, I never missed a word he said, all the years I had known him. Unfortunately, Bill, died nine years later, he was only thirty two years old. Bill was just one of the many managers, we had in our department, they were all very nice. Their attitude, more than anything else, helped me to gain confidence on the job.

I had been working in housekeeping for two weeks helping to get the rooms ready for the opening day when one morning, I found Bill in the laundry room surrounded by racks of uniforms.

"I have a surprise for you," he said. "Go to the ninth floor, and look for room two. Ask for Gayle."

I took the elevator to the ninth floor, and as I walked toward the room, I noticed that the door was open, so I walked in. The room was filled with racks of uniforms and sewing machines. I was greeted by three beautiful young girls, Gayle, Deirdre, and Walguria. I couldn't help but notice how young they looked. I knew I was much older than all three of them, but they were very friendly and easy to get along with. Some people might have felt intimidated by so many younger girls, but I didn't—I had spent more than a decade of my working life surrounded by teenage girls much younger than me back home in Jamaica.

We settled down to work on the uniforms with a deadline hanging over our heads: the hotel was due to open in two weeks, and there was a flurry of fittings. But it didn't bother me. I always work best under pressure. I loved the job and I worked long hours of overtime without feeling tired. I had finally found the job of my dreams and I was on cloud nine. Now all I needed to do was to prove myself worthy of the confidence my manager had placed. When I thought of all the people who had applied for the same job, I knew it was a miracle, a blessing from God.

Deirdre, Gayle, and Walguria told me that they had worked at Radio City Music Hall. Not long afterward, Jane, and Yunlan was hired to work as seamstress. Deirdre, a tall, shapely, attractive West Indian girl quickly became my best friend. Soon, we became the leading team to handle all the most complex uniforms. Much later, Marriott decided to downsize the number of employees working as seamstress. Deirdre and Yunlan was transferred to another department, and Jane later retired. At first I felt extremely lonely, but I quickly adjusted. For the next ten years, I remained the lone seamstress on the job.

As usual, I was aware that lipreading requires guesswork and that I could easily misinterpret what someone was saying. I was wearing a hearing aid at the time, but I was aware that it was not reliable for speech. I usually managed to stay focused on the questions that most employees were likely to ask. But then one day a manager from the gift shop came to ask for a suit for one of the mannequins.

"I need a suit for a mannequin," he said, but I thought he was asking for a suit for Manny, one of his employees.

"I have a suit for him," I replied. "But I don't have his inseam" I was about to ask him to let Manny come in to fit his uniform, but his next words sent me reeling.

"Oh," he said, "he is a little taller than me, but he is on a two-step platform." Only then, did I got the clue that he was asking for a suit for a mannequin.

I immediately went and fetched him the smallest size we had in stock. After he left, I had a good laugh at myself. I certainly hope the poor guy never realized I had gotten his words all mixed up.

I was surprised by my ability to communicate with so many employees from so many different cultures. We mostly talked about their uniforms, which made it easier for me, but occasionally they'd talk about the current news. In a way, I felt secure knowing that I was serving a diverse staff. It made me realize that I was just a part of that diversity. Perhaps I was beginning to realize what America was all about: a country where people with many different heritages and beliefs blended together in harmony.

CHAPTER 11

The New York Marriott Marquis

THE NEW YORK Marriott Marquis opened its doors to the public on a sunny day in August 1985. It was a day I will never forget. As I took my seat at the table reserved for my teammates and me, I gazed in wonder at the beautiful Broadway ballroom. A steady stream of employees from every department poured into the ballroom, looking professional and immaculate in their uniforms. I felt a sense of pride knowing I was part of a wonderful team that had worked hard to get those uniforms ready for opening day. It was hard to believe that in less than a month, I had managed to take my place and feel at home among a team of younger girls who quickly became my friends.

Working at the Marriott Marquis on Broadway was completely different from anything I had ever imagined. It didn't take me long to realize that the hotel was truly a model of glamour as well as diversity. Many famous people stayed at the hotel, and I enjoyed the opportunity to meet people from all over the world. Many of our guests shopped while they were in New York and needed alterations on their clothes. Our employees included people from many cultures who spoke many languages. It was truly wonderful to see so many people of different cultures working together as one big happy family. It made me wish the whole world could be as harmonious.

Not long after opening, the huge employee cafeteria was renamed the International Cafe, and Marriott began the custom of serving a variety of cultural dishes annually. Even the **Wall Street Journal** took note. An article by Alex Markels described how Marriott managed its diverse staff and stated the view that diversity could be a competitive advantage. The article said that the hotel had approximately seventeen hundred employees representing every race. They came from seventy countries and spoke forty-seven languages.

When Mike Stengel became the general manager of the Marriott Marquis, I was truly happy for him. He was very personable and was familiar with all the staff members, always taking the time to let employees know how much he valued their work. I think the biggest contribution to Marriott success is the fact that management and employees cooperate. Working there taught me a valuable lesson in teamwork, and I realized that when managers treat employees with respect instead of dictating to them, in return they get better service from the employees.

It didn't take me long to realize that, for cultural and religious reasons, many employees did not like to wear the standard uniforms. Many of the girls also needed maternity uniforms, which was not available. The standard uniforms did not fit some employees properly. So, for many reasons, there was a constant demand for major alterations and custom-made uniforms.

Bill Cullen, who was still my manager, always included me in the decisions-making when it came to the employees uniforms. So I was able to persuade him to order bolts of fabric. As soon as the fabric arrived, I began designing the maternity uniforms for all the girls who needed them. It turned out to be a huge success, and before long, I was making custom uniforms for many of the employees who could not get the proper fit from the standard uniforms. With so many satisfied employees and guests, I became well known in the hotel, and my manager allowed me to make my own decisions.

Less than six months after I began working at Marriott, my husband suffered a stroke. He was on his way to work when he collapsed in the subway on West 46th Street and was rushed to St. Claire Hospital. It was late in the evening when we got a call from the hospital informing us that he had a stroke and was in a coma. Val, Mark, Anne, and I drove to New York. There was nothing I could do except to pray that God would not take Linton away from us. At the hospital, I couldn't bear to see him lying in the hospital bed with so many tubes attached to his frail body. Since the hospital was only a few blocks from where I was working, I was able to visit him twice a day—every morning before I started my shift and in the evening before I left for home.

I thanked God I had such wonderful coworkers who were encouraging. They helped to keep me focused, otherwise I don't know how I would have managed. Linton made a wonderful recovery, and after nine months of physical therapy he was on his feet again. He was barely sixty-two years old, but he never went back to work full time.

With Linton in recovery, I was feeling more much better, and able to devote more time to my job. I was having lunch in the cafeteria one day when Bill came and sat beside me. "You are doing a great job, Elometer," he said. "I really appreciate it. All the managers are aware of the great job you have done on the employees' uniforms."

I was very pleased with the compliment, but I didn't want to appear as if I was proud of my achievements, so I simply said "Thank you, Bill."

I really didn't like group meetings, because it was very difficult for me to understand what was being said. Half the time I couldn't follow the fast-moving lips of the speaker, and it was very discouraging. At the first anniversary celebration, the ballroom was packed with employees, but I managed to get a seat near the front where I could better see the faces of the speakers, but I still missed most of what the first speaker said. I glanced around at the crowd, and noticed a group of about twenty people gathered around a large table. A sign language interpreter was using her hands to translate the words of the speaker. After observing them for a few minutes, I was amazed at how easy it was for the deaf employees to understand what was being said through sign language. I wished I had had the opportunity to learn sign language. For the first time, I understood why deaf people are proud of sign language as part of their culture.

In April 1987, I decided to sell my home in Jamaica and buy a home in Queens. I wanted my children to go to college in New York once they graduated from high school. Mark was attending Middlesex Community College at night and working full time at Merrill Lynch. He was doing very well at his job, but I wanted him to attend college full time. Anne was a brilliant student and I had high hopes for her in college. I knew she could succeed in any subject in college if she put her mind to her studies.

I spent two months renovating the house in New York, then moved in late in June. I looked forward to the move with a heart full of hope, since this was the first time that Linton and I would live together with our children in our own home. After years of living in my brother's home, it was a welcome change.

Linton had been through nearly a year of physical therapy and came out better than expected, but he was very depressed and I hoped that moving to our own home would help to cheer him up. We had been married for nearly twenty years, and most of our married life had been spent apart. So, in a way, I looked forward to starting a new life in my home with my family. When I moved, Mark and Anne stayed at Val's. After three weeks, I was getting discouraged. I couldn't understand why Mark and Anne could not make up their minds to live with me. They had always said that they wanted to live in New York with me, and it really hurt to see their empty room every day. But at least I had Linton for company, or so I thought.

I still hoped that my kids would change their minds and come and live with me. I didn't worry too much about Mark, he was a quiet kid who didn't go out much, and I knew he was safe with Val and could take care of himself. I worried about Anne, though. At seventeen, she was a beautiful young girl, very popular, and had many friends. She was in love with Tracy, a guy she had met in high school and didn't want to move away from her boyfriend. I worried about what she was doing with her life, but I couldn't reason with her about going to college. Being away from my children was the hardest thing in the world for me.

Little did I know that I was facing two and a half years of loneliness and heartbreak, and that was not the end of it. I soon found out that I was in for another nasty surprise. I came home from work late one night to find a packed suitcase and an airline ticket on my bed. Linton stood behind me as I glanced at the ticket. A shock went through me when I realized that he was leaving for Jamaica the next day. I whirled around and said, "When were you going to tell me?" He stood his ground not saying a word. "How long had you been planning this?" I demanded.

After a long pause he said, "My brother, Theo, and I are planning to start a business in Jamaica."

I was shaking inside but I did my best to stay as calm as possible. "Are you planning to live in Jamaica?"

I waited for him to answer but all he said was, "I will come back to visit when I can."

I just couldn't hold back my anger anymore. "Listen, Linton," I said. "If we are going to live apart again, we might as well get a divorce. Haven't we lived apart for most of our married life?"

After Linton left, I felt helpless and my nerves were stretched to the limit. I had a regular telephone but I didn't have a TTY because I never thought I would need one. I never had any relatives or friends who owned a TTY. I had always depended on my brother, my husband, and my children for making important telephone calls. With Linton gone, I was desperate to pick up the telephone and call someone, anyone. I needed someone I could talk to. I had never felt more lost and helpless in my life. I cried myself to sleep that night, and every night after that for a week. I was angry at Linton, angry at my kids, angry at the whole world.

I tried to settle down and take comfort in the fact that I was no longer responsible for anyone but myself. But life was too quiet without my family and I hated it. I missed my kids and would gladly put up with all the craziness just to have them with me.

When I didn't hear from Linton for two months, I tried to contact him, but was always told he wasn't there. A couple of months later I decided to see a lawyer about getting a divorce. I told the lawyer that my husband had abandoned me and that I wanted to file for divorce. He told me I had two choices: I could get the divorce if my husband agreed to sign the divorce papers; or I could get the divorce after my husband had abandoned me for a year or more. I filled out some forms and left.

Nearly three months later, I returned home from work late one night. As I walked toward my house, I noticed that the lights were on. I wondered who could be there, and hoped it was Mark or Ann. I didn't bother to knock, hoping to surprise them, but I was the one who got surprised. Linton was sitting in a chair with a big smile on his face. I didn't even know he had a key. Suddenly it felt good to have him back, and I could barely keep myself from rushing into his arms. Instead, I said, "So you came back."

He smiled, "I am going back tomorrow," My heart sank when he told me that he and his brother had brought a boat in Florida and were leaving for Jamaica two days later. He said he had come back only to get some money to help him pay for the boat. I calmly told him about the divorce papers.

"You either stay here or sign these papers," I said.

He took one look at the papers and said, "Give me a pen."

I was in shock when he took the pen and signed the papers as if our marriage didn't mean anything to him. After he left, I decided not to do anything about the divorce papers that he had signed. I told myself that as long as I didn't take the signed papers to the lawyer they were not legal. I was still hoping that our marriage would have a chance to succeed, so I decided not to do anything with them. I wanted to tear up the papers. I had never wanted the divorce. I kept the divorce papers for as long as I could and when I didn't hear from Linton for more than a year, I went ahead and filed the papers with the lawyer. The divorce came through quicker than I expected. After all, he had nothing to contest. He never wanted a home in America, and Anne, our youngest, was eighteen years old. But I was still unhappy with the divorce, and it bothered me for many years afterward. I really regretted I had taken that step. I had hoped that the marriage vows we had taken would last until death parted us, but that was not to be. Regrettably, that was the end of my marriage, a marriage that lasted twenty-one years, though more than half of them had been spent apart. So much for the happy married life I had hoped for.

In April 1990, after more than two years of living alone in New York, with no hope of resolving my marriage or having my children with me, I moved back to New Jersey and once again took up residence with my brother Val. Living alone was something I could never get accustomed to, and I wanted to be with my children. I had originally planned to sell my home in Queens and buy a home in New Jersey, but after posting a "For rent" sign, I got someone to rent it within a week. It was a tremendous relief to be back in New Jersey with my family, and it was definitely more convenient to get to my job in New York by bus from New Jersey.

Shortly after I moved back to New Jersey, I bought a car. Getting around in Kendall Park was not like New York where I had the convenience of taking the train, busses, and taxis. I had to face the fact that my children were all grown up and going their separate ways. I felt I had to take charge of my life, and driving around the countryside gave me the feelings of freedom. As a mother I never wanted to let go, but I realized my children were no longer kids, they wanted to make their own decision and there were nothing I could do about it.

I was aware that Marriott had began hiring people with disabilities, not long after I started working there. I was told that twenty percent of the employees were deaf. As an oral speaking person who did not know sign language, unfortunately, I couldn't communicate with any of the deaf employees, except with a few gesture I knew. One day, a housekeeping manager brought in a pretty young girl for a fitting. She explained to me that the girl was deaf and unable to speak. She then asked me to take her measurements for her uniform. The young girl looked unhappy and embarrassed. I wished I knew how to communicate with her, but there was very little I could do beyond using the gesture used by most hearing people. I smiled, beckoned her to follow me to the fitting room, and offered the dress. "It will look beautiful on you," I wrote on a piece of paper but it was obvious that she didn't understand. The next day, I saw her with a group of other deaf employees and she was happily signing. I was happy for her. After all, human communication is the one of the most important things in our lives.

Some months later, I met Debbie Ciraolo, a sign language interpreter hired by Marriott to help deaf employees to understand what was being said in staff meetings. I was hoping to persuade her to use text message on the billboard. I asked her, "Why don't you use text message on the billboard where everyone can read it?" Debbie told me that English was a second language for most of the deaf employees, and that many of them would not be able to understand the text message. She told me she was hired to interpret words in sign language for them, even though they came from different speaking countries. I was filled with admiration for Debbie. How she managed to sign for such a diverse group is still a mystery to me.

Nineteen ninety-five was a wonderful year for me It was the year my daughter, Anne got married. It was also the year my granddaughter, Sherice, was born. I must have been the happiest mother on earth when Anne told me that she was getting married. Anne and Tracy had met in High School, they had been friends for eight years, and I was happy that they had finally decided to marry. Since the wedding would take place in nine months, and I was still working, I began planning right away. The very next day, I drove around the city, looking for a fabric store. There were not many of them in Kendall Park. As I drove home, memories of Anne as a little girl, kept coming back to me. I remember her sweet little face as she came home from school each day, throwing her little arms around me.   For just one precious moment I felt like I was losing my daughter, but then I realized that I was not losing my daughter. I was gaining a son, and Tracy was a faithful and wonderful person, a welcome addition to my family.

Although I had began working on the wedding dress three months before the wedding, I had many set-backs. I had very little time to spare, when one of the six bridesmaids asked me to make her dress, because she could not get a dress in her size. The biggest problem was that the bridesmaids' dresses had lots of beadings, sequins, and rhinestones that had to be sewn on by hand.

The day of the wedding arrived. It was a beautiful sunny August day. The church was packed with over two hundred guest. I felt such pride as I watched my beautiful daughter walking down the aisle. The reception that followed, lasted well into the night. Attended by many of my relatives and friends, I watched my daughter as she danced with her husband and then went off on their honeymoon.

The only disappointment was the photographer, that Anne, and Tracy, had chosen to take the wedding pictures. The photographer had offered a discount if I paid her in advance. I did, but she failed to deliver the photographs and we had nothing but amateur photographs.

In 1996, I enrolled in a course at the American Sign Language Institute. It was very encouraging that many of the managers and human resources personnel, at Marriott were also learning sign language. I will never forget the feeling of fear that gripped me when I was told that I would not be permitted to use speech during classes. We were told never to use our voices but to be silent and learn to communicate by signing. The session was conducted by a young graduate student from Gallaudet University, who made it clear that he was not a speaking person. All the teachers were deaf, beautiful intelligent young people. It was wonderful to watch them communicate with their hands in such an easy and stress-free manner. I was surprised to find that I was the only student with hearing loss in the class of twenty students. After watching for two hours in silence, and trying to communicate with my hands, I was caught up in the wonder of signing as I had never experienced it before. As I left the building that day I saw the huge poster hanging outside the entrance door. It summed up everything I wanted to say. It read in part. "You are now entering the world of the deaf. After you have been there, the world will never look the same." And that was certainly true for me.

After attending classes for a week, I had the opportunity to interview one of my

teachers, a very intelligent and efficient young man named Paul. He wrote English so well that I was convinced that he must be able to speak English too. He could lip-read, but he let me know that he could only say two words in English (thank you). He was very accommodating and wrote on the blackboard that he was the only one with hearing loss in his family. He had never heard the sound of speech but he had learned to read and write.

After attending classes for three months I was discouraged and felt that I had learned very little. I wanted to learn as much as possible, but I realized that sign language is best learned from childhood. I knew it would take years for me to learn to communicate with my hands. Like many hearing people, I realized that there are many thing we as a society can do to communicate with someone who can't hear. We don't have to go to school to learn a few basic signs. Signing, after all, is not strange to hearing people. I have seen hearing people cue each other all the time, across crowded rooms, in churches, at funerals, and in other public places. They gesture and mouth words without giving it a second thought. I often wonder if hearing people are aware that those same signs can come in handy to cue someone who is unable to hear. People who cannot hear our voices are visually oriented. They respond to things they can see, touch, or feel. It is really a pity that so many people in our society fail to realize that hearing loss have nothing to do with intelligence.

CHAPTER 12

A Family Affairs

A
S I WRITE this final chapter, I realized how truly blessed I am. It's a long way from the lonely farm life, and the years I spent in isolation. Accepting my destiny after I lost my hearing, was a challenge for me, and the only way I could overcome it was by having confidence in myself. Had I spent a lifetime dwelling on the negativity of hearing loss, and the effect it had on my life, I would never have become part of the hearing society. One of the most important lesson I have learned , was to acknowledge my limitations.   The way I see, and feel, about myself, made a big difference in my life. God have always been the guiding principle in my life, giving me hope and confidence, to do most of the things I had set my mind on. Without confidence, I could never imagined using a telephone, driving a car, marrying a decent hearing man, and raising two beautiful children. I could never dream of getting a very important position in one of New York's top hotels and getting the respect of those I work with. I feel truly blessed to have met many people from all over the world, and making many friends.

In the fall of 2004, I began thinking about retiring, but it was an agonizing decision I just couldn't make. I loved the job and the people I worked with, but I didn't want to go through another harsh winter, making the long commute between New Jersey and New York. I had worked through several long snowy winters, and I was prone to catching cold in the winter months. I also realized that I had been working for most of my life, with little or no time off for my family. I had been to the funerals of so many relatives and friends, it made me realize how uncertain life can be. The deaths of my father in 1998, and my ex-husband Linton in 2004, had a profound effect on me. After Lincoln suffered a stroke—his second in eighteen years—the hospital sent him to a nursing home, where he was very unhappy. Every time I visited, he kept begging me to take him home. When he was permitted to leave, I cut my work hours to three days a week, so I could take care of him. Lucky for me, Nohemy, one of my coworker was able to work on my days off. I wanted Linton to be as comfortable as possible during his last days on earth. Thank God, he wasn't in pain, and he was able to walk. Although our marriage did not last, "until death us do part," we did know peace and love in the end. I am glad I was there for him.

Sadly, it was at Linton's funeral that I met most of his family, including his nephews Trevor, Zak, and Roland, their wives, and their children. I had met Linton's nephew Joseph some years before, and I must give him credit for bringing the rest of the family to us. I wish I had met them many years before.

Leaving my job at Marriott was not an easy decision to make, but it was a decision I knew I would have to make, eventually. I had six weeks of vacation time, so I decided to take a month off from my job. I wrote a letter to Mike Stengel, I wanted him to be the first to know of my intention to retire, and to thank him and the company for the privilege of working there.

I was very grateful when Mike invited me and my family, to have lunch with him and his family, along with some of my coworkers. Unfortunately, his wife Karen, was unable to attend. It was a wonderful lunch and afterward I was presented with a huge framed card, signed by many grateful employees. Their beautiful words brought tears to my eyes. It was an emotional moment for me, and I knew it would be impossible for me to say goodbye to all of them. I was close to tears. I looked into the faces of everyone standing around me, anxiously waiting for me to say goodbye or something. I was close to tears and couldn't find the words. One, by one, I called their names. Finally I said, "You know how hard it is for me to say goodbye." I pleaded, "Let's not say goodbye. I will just say, 'see you in a little while.' That really broke the spell and saved me from having to make an otherwise heartbreaking goodbye.

Since leaving Marriott, some of my coworkers; mainly, Nohemy, Blanca, Erma, Nancy, David, and Maria, have faithfully kept in touch with me. We get together at least every summer, and we always have lots of fun when we meet. I wish I could name each, and every one of my friends, and coworkers, but they are too many to mention. I think of them as my family, and they are always a reminder that family do not have to be blood-related. They are true friends, who I knew will always be there for me, in good times as well as bad.

After almost four years in retirement, I have adjusted to the quiet suburban lifestyle in Kendall Park, where I bought my home. When the weather is good, I go for long walks, sometimes with my friend Lynn Boardman. I met Lynn some years ago while taking the bus to work in New York. She is a devoted Christian, and one of the most honest persons I have ever met. We often go places and shopping together.

My aim is to be as active as possible in my retirement. Some years ago, I had joined Christ the King, an Evangelical Lutheran church near my home. Unfortunately, I wasn't able to understand much of the sermons and I hoped that the church would provide captioned text. Pastor, Fred Schott, was very considerate of my needs and gave me a printed copy of the sermon each Sunday. I was really grateful, but reading the text and following what was being said wasn't easy. I have since, discovered that there are lots of captioned sermons on television, which is more relaxing, and easy to follow.

Today, I am grateful for my loving family. My son, Mark, my daughter, Anne, my brother, Val, my son-in-law, Tracy, and my two beautiful grandchildren, Tracy Jr. and Sherice. I feel truly blessed when my family are with me; I appreciate them more than ever. My children and grandchildren have always been the driving force in my life. They are truly a blessing from God. My daughter Anne, and her family moved to South in the summer of 2009. Saying goodbye to them was heartbreaking. I missed them so much. But we have always kept in touch.

Writing this book was really an adventure for me. It was like rediscovering myself . In fact it was more like a healing therapy an, adventure into my life and my relationship with those I care about. I have learned to understand myself and my family better, and to be more forgiving. But I must also confess that it was a very painful experience to write about some of the things in my life. I had to do lots of soul-searching in order to be fair to everyone. For the first time in my life, I realized that my family had very little experience with hearing loss. They did what they thought was best for me. My father was the first person who told me about God, and I will always be grateful to him for helping to establish my faith in God. I firmly believe that whatever has happened to me in the past was my destiny. In spite of everything, I know, my family cared about me. It took   heartbroken decisions for me to do many of the things I did, but in the end I came to realized that love have many faces.

Conclusion

I T IS MY sincere hope that the readers of this book, will be able to get a better understanding of hearing loss, and the world in which we live. Most hearing people I have met are very compassionate, and willing to help those in need. I would like to point out that many deaf people who use sign language and live within the culture are perfectly happy with their lives as it is. They view deafness as a culture to be proud of, and do not see it as a handicap. They are truly a group of confident people who accept deafness , and are proud of it, and it's a right they are entitled to.

To most hearing people, hearing loss is really an "invisible" condition. Unfortunately hearing loss remains the least understood because of communication barriers. My own experience have taught me that very few hearing people really understand the stark horrors of the loss of sounds. By writing this book, I hope to put a human face on deafness, and to be a voice for the voiceless. To show others that deafness is simply the inability to hear. I am confident that once we have gotten the message across, the communication barriers that divides and isolates us, can be overcome with awareness. Throughout this book ,I have tried to show that deafness do not limit a person intelligence, as many people seems to think. My life experience is a living example of that. I can truly say that I have lived two different lives in two completely different worlds. Living in a hearing, and silent world, for me, is as different as night and day.

Technology is changing the world for millions of us and bringing us closer to the hearing world. Never before in the history of the world have we witnessed so many wonderful inventions. The cochlear implant is just one of the many wonderful inventions that is bringing hopes to millions of adults and children with hearing loss. Today, we can communicate with almost anyone, anywhere in the world, through text message. In addition to the National Telephone Relay System, we have the Captioned Telephone and a lots of different ways to communicate. Text message have made it easy for all of us hearing or not to contact friends and relatives anywhere. And there is still a lot of improvement going on every day. But I hope see some improvement in the Closed Captioning television programs. It is not always easy to follow the fast moving, and frequently incorrect text on the screen when watching the news, or a movie. I hope text message will become available wherever vocal announcement are made. We need text message in Churches, Hospitals, Airport and all public places.

One of the most wonderful news for people who are unable to hear the voices of friends and relatives on the phone is the Web Cap Telephone. Available through Hamilton and Sprint, both debuted in the summer of 2009, and are available for use with the internet. The CapTel, as it is called, is a simple telephone equipped with a text screen, that enables people who are deaf or hard of hearing to see every word the caller says right on the telephone. It is also available on the web with a regular telephone and it is free.

I can only hope that my experience will inspire other families, especially those with disabled children, to realize that nothing can be more damaging to a child's self-esteem than to be constantly told, that he, or she, will not be able to go out into the world and live a normal life.

Telling your children that they are destined to a life of failure, is setting them up for a lifetime of struggles, and heartbreak. Children need to be brought up with confidence in themselves; they need encouragement to get ahead in life—especially children with disabilities.

No matter what choices each of us makes in life, we should strive for the best in every decision we make, and above all, give ourselves something to hope for. Many deaf and hard-of-hearing people have made their mark on society. To name just a few of them: Oscar winning actress Marlee Matlin; Heather Whitestone, Miss America 1995; Jack R. Gannon, a wonderful writer and lecturer; and Dr. Robert Davila, who was appointed to the office of Special Education and Rehabilitation Services by President George H. W. Bush in 1989.

We should be aware that people with hearing loss are divided among those who use sign language, and those who speak. It would be a wonderful world, if we could all put aside our cultural differences, and respect each other culture and communications. By sharing and exchanging communication skills, we have everything to gain and nothing to lose.   There are many choices for the parents of deaf children today, and Cued Speech, is one of them. Cued Speech was developed in 1966, by Dr. R. Orin Cornett. Over the years, it has became a very popular educational alternative for deaf children and their hearing parents. Most importantly, Cued Speech work in conjunction with lipreading, and some hand-signing. It is easy to learn and provides deaf children with access to spoken language. It is one of the best method for bridging the communication gap for hearing parents and their deaf child.

Even though, I am very good at understanding speech in normal conversation and enjoy talking with hearing friends. I would never rely on reading lips alone for getting important information; it is much too risky, with too many look-alike words, and having to guess so many words that are invisible on the lips. Sign language is said to be the fourth most popular language in America. It's a true visual language that should be taught in more schools not many hearing people know how to communicate in sign language.

If we could reduce the myths and misconceptions about hearing loss, we would be on the way to bridging the communication gap that divides and isolates us. Let us hope that, like the Berlin Wall, the wall of isolation for all of us will fall down so that we can emerge into the world with confidence and become part of a society in which we all must live and work.